SNAKES, SQUIRRELS & BEARS, OH MY!

Finding Humor Amid Life's Frustrations

To Donna,

Find the humor in life!

Greg Peck
6-10-23

Greg Peck

Copyright © 2023 Greg Peck

All rights reserved.

ISBN-13: 9781949085730

Dedication

Dedicated to my dear wife, Cheryl,
who played a role in many of these stories but,
as I started production of this book in spring 2023,
had moved to a memory care facility.

"We are surrounded by the façade of everyone but us having it together. Thus we find joyful unity in a flop."

--Author Michael Perry in his 2022 book
"Hunker, Brief Essays on Human Connection"

Acknowledgments

Many people supported this project, and I hope I'm not leaving anyone out. Thanks to Christine Keleny of CKBooks Publishing in New Glarus, Wisconsin, for designing the covers, and to former *Janesville Gazette* colleague Dan Lassiter for enhancing my self-portrait on the front. Also, thanks to author Jerry Apps for writing a back-cover blurb, as he did on my first two books.

Thanks to fellow authors Robb Grindstaff for his introduction and Michael Perry for allowing use of a poignant quote from one of his most-recent books.

My brother Ed Peck and his staff at Filament Marketing in Madison, Wisconsin, enhanced the resolution of interior photos, and my brother Tom Peck helped figure out a formatting glitch.

Members of my writing group through the years—John Halverson, Ed Timmer, Don Allison, and the late Den Adler—deserve credit for suggesting improvements to my early drafts.

Likewise, my sister, Karen Benesch, and friend and librarian Barb Husch get kudos for offering feedback on these stories. Finally, thanks to sister-in-law Candice Reed for proofreading them, and to former *Gazette* colleagues Shawn Sensiba and Barb Uebelacker for proofing advance copies of the book. Any remaining errors are my fault.

Contents

Introduction	1
1. Just Short of Road Rage at the Checkout Aisles	4
2. Surviving Childhood Bowls of Sugar	7
3. How Technology Drives Me Nuts	10
4. Getting Squirrelly	16
5. Hair Today, Gone Tomorrow	20
6. Remembering Our Sweet Little Travel Companion	23
7. A Snake Beside the Frozen Steaks	26
8. Nuts, Just Minimum Wage	30
9. "This Is Only a Test"	32
10. How I Wed on My Birthday	36
11. Fear? Not!	41
12. Sad Saga of a Sagging Sofa	43
13. Rental Car Recoil	47
14. Just Like Animals	51
15. A Granddaughter's Worldly Wisdom	53
16. Coming to Blows with a Snowblower	55
17. How Wet?	60
18. Boat Be Gone	62
19. Customer "Service" Is a Contradiction in Terms	66
20. I "Bearly" Slept a Wink!	72
21. One Sneaky Snake	75
22. Friend's Foibles Put the Fun in Fishing	78
23. In the Kitchen, It's Too Hot or Too Cold	82
24. Molly's Frightening First Night	85
25. Rummaging into the Human Psyche	90
26. Please Stop if You See Me Stranded by the Road	94
27. When the IRS Wants a Chunk of You	99
28. Six Things That Could Go Wrong When Remodeling (Your Results May Vary)	101
29. The Tale of Todd	108
30. Everything Came Up Roses	110
31. Children's Heavy Equipment Exhausts Grandparents	117
32. Lesson in Liquid Propane	119
33. Walks to Remember	123

34. Don't Fall for It	125
35. I'd Be "Bearly" Fast Enough	130
36. Keep the Faith: Packer Fans Are Everywhere	132
37. Retrieving a Wedding Gift in the Nick of Time	135
38. Free-for-All at the Little Free Library	138
39. Ease Is Not in the Bag	143
40. It's the Curse of Christmas	145
41. Detective Apprehends Golf Club Thief	149
42. Yes, It's Called Yard Work, So Get Busy	152
43. Serving Breakfast and Warm Smiles	155
44. Sister Puts the "Ho Ho Ho" in the Holidays	159
45. Reports of My Demise…	162
46. A Dose of Reality	164

Introduction

Greg Peck and I have a lot in common, it seems. We both had careers in the community newspaper business, including time overlapping in Wisconsin newspapers. I ended up affiliated with *The Janesville Gazette*, the newspaper where Greg spent much of his career, although he had recently retired when I came on board.

Our paths never crossed until we met at a Wisconsin Writers Association conference in Appleton. I'd been writing and editing fiction for many years. Greg had published a book about a 1927 wedding-day tragedy that befell a couple married in his hometown of Marshall, Wisconsin, and was planning a second book on growing up in that small town. He was also tackling the idea of writing a novel. Yet another thing we shared.

We hit it off at the conference and discovered our common background. When Greg invited me to join a writing critique group that met monthly in Janesville, I jumped at the chance. In addition to Greg and me, the group included John, Ed, and Denny. The five of us met at Denny's house to share stories we were working on, encourage each other, and support each other's writing habits with detailed, constructive critiques on how to make them better. But the main byproduct of these sessions was the friendship.

I soon retired from the newspaper business, and my wife and I relocated to the Ozark hills and lakes of Missouri. I swear I'm not distributing drugs or laundering money for the cartel.

Reading stories in this collection reminded me of something else we had in common—something I wouldn't have thought was similar until I'd spent a few years in Wisconsin.

Having grown up in the southern United States, I'd always imagined the northern states to be quite different from what I knew best, places such as North Carolina, Oklahoma, and Texas. I didn't have to be in Wisconsin long to discover the similarities in people, in culture, in lifestyle, but especially in daily life experiences.

I marveled at how alike Wisconsin is to Texas. Milwaukee is Houston, the huge and diverse metropolis with all the amenities and all the problems endemic to big cities. Madison is Austin, the seat of government, home to the largest state university, music, entertainment, food, and youthful exuberance and idealism.

The rest of each state is largely rural, agricultural, small cities, and smaller towns. Hunting, fishing, camping, pickup trucks, and country music. Communities where everyone knows everyone, and a helping hand is as common as a wave from the farmer driving the tractor five miles per hour on the county highway. Farmers markets, fish fries, high school football, and family supper at the local bar or restaurant.

Faith. Church on Sunday, although in Texas it's more Baptist and Methodist, whereas Wisconsin leans Catholic and Lutheran.

This story collection—written over more than a decade and not printed chronologically—captures those moments in perfect photographs in the mind. These slice-of-life stories are intensely relatable, regardless of your age or background, whether you're from Wisconsin or Texas or New Jersey. The dry wit might bring a smile or a laugh-out-loud moment. The conversational voice makes it feel like the author is a good friend, even if you've never met Greg, as he tells you about his day over a cup of coffee or a cold, adult beverage. Often humorous, always tender, and with a keen eye for the routine, even mundane moments that give us our shared humanity. Nostalgic at times, whether it's reminiscing about some childhood moment years earlier or a visit to the grocery store yesterday.

I frequently found myself thinking, "I've had that exact same experience," but I hadn't thought of it in years, and possibly missed the poignancy or humor in it at the time—whether struggling to remodel the house or repair the car, dealing with the complexities of a grandchild's car seat or the frustrations of a slow cashier lane.

The stories and the writing carry that feel of a familiar weekly newspaper columnist, which comes naturally to Greg, of course. I

SNAKES, SQUIRRELS & BEARS, OH MY!

often thought of Lewis Grizzard, Dave Barry, or Erma Bombeck as I both devoured and savored these little nuggets of life.

—Robb Grindstaff, author of four novels, fiction editor and writing coach. His most recent novels are "Slade" and "Turning Trixie."

1
Just Short of Road Rage at the Checkout Aisles

You don't want to be ahead of me at the grocery store's checkout line. Patience isn't one of my virtues.

I do the shopping in our household. It has always been that way. My wife does the laundry; I get the groceries. We struck that deal before we wed.

For me, getting groceries is no leisure activity. It's get in, get out, as fast as possible. I'm all but running down some aisles. It's annoying when someone angle parks a shopping cart and studies the shelves as if doing an Indiana Jones probe for the Holy Grail, oblivious to the fact that he or she has blocked my path.

Oh, I'll stop and visit with someone I know. My wife, Cheryl, calls me "Mr. Social." I enjoy chatting with people I know and like. If I spot one of the few people in the world I dislike, I'll skip that aisle, avoid that person, and double back later. And if I don't know you, I have no reason to talk other than to be cordial and try not to show my frustration as you apologize when you realize your haphazardly parked cart impedes my progress.

But woe to the slow person at the checkout line.

I approach checkout aisles with trepidation. Like most shoppers, I'll scan them to choose the shortest one. I even guess possible speeds of those in line based on appearances and the numbers of items in their carts. If first impressions don't pan out, or if a sudden holdup slows progress up front—"Joe Bob, can I get a price check on Tidy Bowl?"—I'll switch to another line.

I try to avoid the three worst habits of checkout decorum. You probably know the types.

First, there's the crazed coupon clipper. Heck, I clip coupons, too, but I'm talking about the person who tries to slip in coupons for products not purchased and others that have expired. As the checkout gal studies and rejects them, she's spending time and I'm tapping my foot.

Second is the little old lady who, instead of handing over a fifty for $46.89 worth of groceries, is counting small bills and then starts mining the bottom of her cluttered, gunny-sack-like purse for coins—down to the last penny. Time I'm wasting waiting and waiting.

Third is the guy who thinks the checkout boy wants to hear about his kidney stone or the gal who believes the female clerk simply must hear about her new poodle.

Woe to me if someone doubles up and harbors two of these disturbing habits.

Such was the case the other day. I'm in more than the usual hurry. It's early afternoon, a rain-dappled Saturday, and chats with two favorite coworkers—one current, one retired—slow me down. But I have to start the night shift at 4, and I don't want to spend the rest of my precious, dwindling time at the store.

Now, I study the checkout options. The pickings aren't pretty. Several shoppers wait in each aisle. I pick one I think will be fastest.

Wrong again.

The clerk seems a tad lacking in hand-eye coordination as she scans items. I grab *Reader's Digest* from the rack. I review the table of contents and spot two stories of interest. I start reading one, skip to the other, and glance up.

Oh, oh. Seems we've lost our bag boy. Did he leave to use the bathroom? Jump over to some other aisle without a bagger? Run for a price check?

Thankfully, the couple whose groceries are going through the scanner aren't standing idle. The woman is starting to bag their goods. I consider joining her to expedite the process as products pile up. I see the checkout boy returning. He's got a bottle of something for the last customer, who's waiting with a cartload.

Finally, with just one person ahead of me, I put the magazine back. But this woman seems to have habit Number 3. She's waving her hand

and engaging the clerk in conversation, telling her all about her physical therapy. Oh, boy. Progress crawls.

I retrieve the magazine. I gaze at the guy behind me.

"Seems we picked the wrong aisle," I suggest.

"Seems you're right."

I start reading again. I'm finishing the story and glance up. The customer is continuing her dramatic saga, and her total tops $100. She's handing over big bills, then starts counting singles. Oh, oh. Annoying habit Number 2, too. What's worse, now she has just ten bucks and change left to pay, and she's digging in her purse for a debit card.

Painful to watch. Even more painful to be waiting behind.

She finally finishes telling her life story, is on her way, and I roll my cart to the front.

"Hi, how are you?" the clerk says courteously.

"Fine," I say succinctly, trying not to start a conversation that will drag this out but also trying not to be terse or expose my annoyance.

I grab the big, heavy objects off the bottom rack of my cart. Maybe she'll get the hint that I'm in a hurry. She seems to pick up the pace. Hopeful.

She rips through fast, then trims the staggering price total with my clutch of coupons. I pay cash and am ready to fly.

"Do you want a drive-up?"

"No," I say. Too slow, I think to myself.

Now, however, it's raining harder. I quickly load my groceries, return the cart, and hop in.

I take my usual getaway route—except, whoops—street work is blocking that exit. I steer into the store's side lot to whip a U-turn. I'm doubling back to the stop sign when, out of my peripheral vision, I catch the flash of a red sports car, some guy thinking he's Mario Andretti. I slam on the brakes just in time.

"Hey!" I shout, but of course with our windows rolled up, I'm yelling to myself. "What's the big hurry?"

2
Surviving Childhood Bowls of Sugar

A list of my favorite boyhood breakfast cereals reads like a parent's worst nightmare. Most often, my overdoses of sugar came from Kellogg's with its Apple Jacks, Froot Loops, Cocoa Krispies, and Frosted Flakes; and Cinnamon Toast Crunch from General Mills. Pitch Post's Super Sugar Crisp and Alpha-Bits into the mix, and add the occasional box of Quaker Oats Cap'n Crunch, which made the Environmental Working Group's top ten list of the sweetest offenders in a 2011 study. Each bowl served up a whopping 44.4 percent sugar. Apple Jacks and Fruit Loops didn't rank much better, both at more than 41 percent. The study suggested that many children's cereals contained more sugar than some desserts.

Back in the 1960s, if our cupboard ran short of cereals before Mom's next trip to Bergholz Grocery in the Dane County, Wisconsin, village of Marshall, it wasn't a problem. I'd bust up a mittful of the ever-present Graham Crackers and dump a couple spoonsful of sugar on top, then drench them with milk.

If one bowl was good, two or even three were better, right? You'd think I would've been the sweetest kid in the classroom.

These cereals also made great after-school and nighttime snacks as I gobbled handfuls of sweetness right from the box until it was empty. My parents probably single-handedly paid my dentist's green fees because every time I visited his dreaded office in nearby Waterloo, I needed two cavities drilled and filled.

Thank God some of that study's top ten didn't exist back when I burned off some of that sugar on my weekday walks to school.

Reading the backs of those boxes—or digging to the bottom to fetch the Super Ball or some other trinket before my older sister got her grubby fingers on it—was almost as enjoyable as my daily dose of sugar. Why, back in the day, I could collect one of three 33 rpm records by the Jackson 5 by clipping it off the back of a Super Sugar Crisp box.

I enjoyed the opportunities to get groceries with Mom. She let me study the boxes and decide which one had the best prize or most interesting back, many featuring mazes, crossword puzzles, and "Can you spot it?" brain teasers. While wolfing down all that sugar, it's a wonder I ever finished any such puzzle.

Those boxes also served as miniature fortresses, blocking the annoying stares and glares of my aforementioned sister, especially if we were in the midst of a childhood feud over lord knows what major transgression.

Oh, those were the days. They came pouring back to me on a recent trip to that same sister's house. Karen lets my wife, Cheryl, and me stay with her when we drive north to visit Mom, who lives nearby. Mom has a cat, and I have cat allergies, so Karen's hospitality is welcome.

Often, Karen makes a breakfast treat for us, such as scones or banana bread. When she doesn't, I dig through her pantry for a box of cereal. On this particular day, I was crunching down on a bowl of Post's Great Grains when I started reading the back of the box. "Absolutely delicious," it said, and Post got no argument from me.

"Heart healthy," it read, adding that "…diets low in saturated fat and cholesterol may reduce the risk of heart disease." Sounds good, I thought, and continued reading.

"A good source of fiber." Noted.

A little square stated that the product was verified by the Non-GMO Project, meaning the cereal is free of organisms whose DNA was manipulated to give them new traits. A little heavy for this early in the morning, but okay.

"Made with 23 grams of whole grains per serving." And "Every bowl contains 10 essential vitamins and minerals." So, great grains.

However, in cruising the Internet while writing this piece, I stumbled across a surprising story. It seems a federal judge certified a class-action lawsuit filed against Post Foods by customers who claimed the company's sugar contents misled consumers. The lawsuit's website went live in 2020. Among the cereals listed were Alpha-Bits and none other than Great Grains. Post Consumer Brands later agreed to pay consumers up to $15 million and to quit using certain terms, including "no high fructose corn syrup," on its cereals containing 10 percent or more of calories from sugars.

A 2019 Stacker report listed the sugar content of Great Grains with raisins, dates, and pecans at 24 percent, including brown sugar, regular sugar, and corn syrup. Well, having somehow lived to Medicare age despite ingesting so much cereal with much more sugar per bowl, I'm thinking I can stomach 24 percent.

Guess I'll pour another bowl.

3
How Technology Drives Me Nuts

The ordeal started on a warm Saturday in October. My wife, Cheryl, and I were headed to Illinois to visit our grandkids and their parents. Said parents—Cheryl's son Adam and his wife, Jill—had purchased Cheryl's cell phone and for years paid her fees to be on Adam's AT&T work account. But when they switched to a bigger data plan, the price doubled. Adam didn't want to pay that much for a phone Cheryl rarely used.

I understood and figured we'd just have them convert the phone to an inexpensive Tracfone service that kept the same number. We were across the Illinois border, into Flatland country, when I realized Cheryl didn't have her purse—and her cell phone was in that purse.

Being a technology doofus, I almost steered off the road at the thought of making this switch myself. I should have turned around, regardless of tolls already amassed. But I drove on.

Jill handed me a Tracfone SIM kit. I thought it meant she had bought us a service package. I should have asked questions when she said it only cost $1. Turns out it contained little computer chips for various service providers.

"Just take it to Target, where I bought it, and they can install it and get Cheryl's phone switched."

If only life were that simple. If only I lived in the Stone Age, when people communicated with grunts and smoke signals and cave drawings, no tech support needed.

I slept little Sunday night, fearing what lie ahead.

That Monday, a Target clerk called for another clerk named Brian. Brian switched to the Verizon SIM card, saying that Verizon's service was our best bet. Okay, I thought.

"You'll need to call to activate the card," he told me.
"What? You can't do that?"
"No."
I left with fear and dread. I had no clue how much fear and dread were appropriate.
At home I worked the Tracfone website until the point where it wanted the serial number on Cheryl's phone. I called Jill.
"Turn on Cheryl's phone."
"Okay."
"What does it say?"
"It shows some service thing with an option to 'continue.'"
"No, no, get to the desktop."
"It won't let me."
"What do you mean?"
"I can't get rid of this thing."
"Oh. Since you've already put the SIM in, the phone is locked. Go back to Target and have them reinstall the AT&T card."
"What?!"
"The guy at Target should have turned on the phone before switching cards. He didn't do that, and the phone is locked. We can't get the information we need."
I kicked and threw objects on my way to the car. I imagined Target Brian thinking "What an idiot" as he mumbled and reversed cards.
I stood in a line of customers awaiting Target Brian's help. His apparently technologically incompetent fellow clerk straightened and dusted shelves.
Finally, I reached Brian, and he made the switch back.
"I suppose I'll need to return a third time to have you reinstall the new SIM, eh?"
"You can do that yourself."
"How?"
"Poke a pin in this little hole, pry the old one out, and slide the new one in."
Seemed simple. I returned home and tried to calm down while eating lunch. Then I texted Jill, but she didn't respond. I figured she was busy at work. I texted again. "Are we going to try changing Cheryl's cell phone over tonight?"

"Tied up the rest of the night. But you can find the instructions online."

"I don't know the previous account details. Please call when you have time."

"You can always try Adam."

I studied the website again. "I got nowhere, so if Adam has time, please have him call," I texted. "Thanks."

Adam didn't call.

Tuesday morning, Jill texted me while I was raking. By the time I found the message, her window of opportunity was almost past. "Gotta do it now then," she texted. "Grab her phone so I can unlock it."

I called, and Jill "unlocked" Cheryl's and mine, which was also tied to Adam's work system. I wasn't sure why it was necessary to also unlock mine and feared it might trigger another catastrophe down the road, but okay.

I then pried the tiny SIM card out using the end of a paper clip. Here's where Doofus took center stage. I wondered why the previous card had a nice bracket but the new one didn't. I slipped the new card into the slot. It didn't seat properly. I tried retrieving it and at one point had it re-emerging at an angle. I should have gotten a tweezers or long-nosed pliers to pull it out. Instead, I tucked it back in and hoped it would fall out straight. It didn't. I gently tapped the phone on the desk, hoping the card would fall out. It only slid in deeper!

During this ordeal, I bumped the old SIM and bracket, and the card fell out. I then realized I was supposed to *attach* the new card to the bracket before sliding it into the slot.

How stupid can a guy be? Will it ever come out, or did I destroy the phone?

I went to see Target Brian, who probably thought I was some Halloween ghoul. I considered blaming this gaffe on my wife, who stayed in the car, but couldn't bring myself to do so.

"Can you get it out?"

"I don't think so. You might have to take it to the uBreakiFix store. They'll probably need to pry open the phone to get it out."

I felt dizzy and saw dollar signs.

"Where is this store?"

"Right across Highway 14."

We drove past the storefronts along Highway 14 but didn't find it. I couldn't look up the address on *my* cell phone because it was back home charging.

I stopped at the nearby AT&T store, where staffers had helped me with phone problems.

"Can't fix that," a service guy said. "Take it to the uBreakiFix store."

"Exactly where *is* that?"

"Right behind Buffalo Wild Wings," he said, pointing out the window.

I circled the restaurant and didn't find the store. I drove down the street to another shopping center, and we finally found it.

"Geez, if either guy had said it was near the UPS store or Taco John's or Panera Bread, I'd have known where it was," I told Cheryl. "It's not on Highway 14, and it's not 'just behind Buffalo Wild Wings.'"

I entered the store, and a bubbly young woman emerged from behind a wall. I explained the problem. "Bet you haven't seen one like this."

"Oh, I've seen some real doozies," she said, never acknowledging whether some other dim bulb had ever done something as ignorant. I imagined the woman and her coworkers guffawing behind the wall. "I can fix that," she said cheerfully. "But I'll have to take the phone apart."

"How much?"

"About $29 before tax."

"How long?"

"Fifteen minutes."

"Can I wait?"

"Sure."

I walked out $31.64 poorer. At least the new SIM was in the bracket and seated properly! I felt hopeful.

Back home, I tried the website again. At one point, for some unexplainable reason, I got Cheryl's phone to call our landline and even talked to Cheryl when she answered. Before I could call another number, a computer voice prompted me to buy air time and get a PIN. Using my credit card, I invested $15.

But when I again tried using Cheryl's phone, I got this message: "You are roaming. To call your mobile carrier or any other number, purchase a calling PIN by pressing 1 now."

"I just *did* that," I shouted into the phone.

I explained this to Jill by text.

"I have nothing. I've never used a Tracfone."

During another fitful night's sleep, it dawned on me: I probably need to plug in the PIN on Tracfone's website! On Day 3, I also couldn't get the site to accept Cheryl's phone's "serial number," which contained numbers and letters. It accepted numbers, but not letters.

Befuddled, I thought to stop at Verizon's office. After all, I was trying to use their service, so someone there should help, right?

A staffer pointed out that it wasn't the "serial number" I needed but, if I scrolled down—Didn't know I could!—I'd find something called the IMEI. Yes, all numbers!

Once home, I again ran into roadblocks when the website requested previous provider details I didn't know.

That evening, Adam asked me to text him a photo of the Tracfone card. I did.

Soon he responded, "Okay, so she will need a new number. Log onto the website and select one. This is because AT&T has already canceled it. From there you need an airtime service plan."

"What? I already have a PIN after buying air time last night."

I went to the website and plugged in that PIN. "Now it is telling me my PIN is invalid," I texted. "The nightmare continues. When I paid for that PIN, I was using Cheryl's phone. Should I assume it's tied to her previous number and is defunct because she'll have a different number?"

Finally, on Day 4, Adam told me my assumption was probably correct. So I returned to Tracfone's website and found the cheapest annual plan—without automatic renewal—$133.57, including tax. It gave Cheryl 1,500 minutes of calling time and 1,500 minutes of texting. She might use 100 of each. I wanted something modest, less expensive.

The website then prompted me to turn off and turn on Cheryl's phone and try making a call. "If it doesn't work, reboot and try again in a few minutes." I tried a call and got the annoying "You are roaming" message. I hung up and spewed expletives on my way upstairs, telling Cheryl I was "done with this."

A few minutes later, two texts pinged Cheryl's phone. One said, "Welcome to Tracfone" and gave her new number. The other urged me to dump more money into a "Mobile Protect" plan. Like I was about to fall for that.

Adam also advised me to call Tracfone and ask for a refund on my initial airtime/PIN purchase. But a hard-to-understand gentleman assured me twice that he saw no such charge from Tracfone.

I wasn't convinced. The morning of Day 5, I called my credit card company and learned I indeed was charged $15 for the first PIN. I explained that I couldn't use it and wanted a refund. After fifteen minutes of back and forth, we finished. A message soon said the charge was dropped.

That same day, Cheryl's phone got a message saying, "The number you use with this iPhone recently changed. Update the trusted phone number you use with your Apple ID so you always have access to your account."

Another pitch for money? I had no clue. I called Adam. Twice.

While awaiting a response, Cheryl and I ate lunch. We watched a squirrel sneak into the live trap and make off with the bait I used to relocate chipmunks.

"That squirrel is like a metaphor for my technology troubles," I said.

"How do you mean?"

"He grabs my nuts, escapes, and leaves me frustrated."

4
Getting Squirrelly

Maybe the bad karma began when I was a teenager and plunked a few squirrels with my .22 rifle.

Maybe it came when I laughed because my wife got upset about hitting a squirrel with her car.

Or the time I caught a squirrel instead of a chipmunk in a live trap and released it in a park two miles from its relatives.

Whatever the case, squirrels continue to be a pain in my butt or, in this case, the shuck in my nut.

They gobble birdseed out of our feeders faster than the cardinals, chickadees, and finches do.

When we put in new sidewalks, some rodent with a bushy tail scampered across the concrete, leaving little footprints with ridges just tall enough to stop the shovel and rattle my wrists after each snowfall.

Squirrels dig up fresh turf every time I try to patch a hole in the lawn.

Two incidents stand out even more.

One came when I owned a Wisconsin Rapids house surrounded by pines in central Wisconsin. I came home one day to strange sounds and found a squirrel in the house. It had eaten through cardboard in the garage that covered an old pipe hole from a wood-burning stove.

The panic-stricken varmint raced around the living room as I tried to herd it out the open front door. It leaped from carpeted floor to furnishings and back again. Then, right there on the family Bible, sitting atop the coffee table, nature called.

Relieved, the squirrel made its way back into the wild without further damage.

Then came the time my wife, Cheryl, was gone for the weekend and I was showering in the basement. After turning off the water, I'll be darned if I didn't hear what sounded like a squirrel scampering across the kitchen linoleum.

"Naw," I told myself. "Must be one in the gutter outside. Must just sound like it's in the kitchen."

Soon I was ready to relax and watch a ballgame on television.

But I noticed the folding glass doors to the gas fireplace were popped open. Next to them, a stuffed teddy bear had tumbled from its perch on a miniature rocking chair.

Squirrels are furry-tailed acrobats that can steal lots of food intended for birds.

"Those idiot boys," I said to myself, recalling the beer party Cheryl's sons threw while I was away the previous evening. "Why were they messing with the fireplace?"

After I settled in with a cold one on the couch, something rustled in the fireplace.

I walked over, stooped, and peered inside. Sure enough, two beady little eyes stared back at me.

"Damn."

Two ideas crossed my mind. Start the fireplace and chase the intruder out the top of the chimney from whence it came, or wait for Cheryl to get home and see if she had a better suggestion.

I opted for the latter, and as you might have guessed, she was appalled at the former.

"You'll wind up frying him," Cheryl said. "It would be cruel and stink to high heaven. Let's just open the front door, pop open the fireplace doors, and hopefully he'll see the light."

I wasn't so confident. Besides, my son was spending the weekend with us.

"If Josh gets bitten by this frightened critter, we'll wind up back in court with the ex," I said.

This isn't one of the squirrels that have invaded my houses, but it must be a relative. Look at that smirk.

While I was frantic, Cheryl remained calm. "So shut the doors to the hallway and kitchen, and I'll sit quietly in the corner and watch to see that he makes his way out," she said. "You two stay in the other room."

"Okay," I said. I handed her my fishing net in case she needed it.

Cheryl's plan worked.

The rat with the fat tail crept out of the fireplace, paused to gaze around, spotted the open front door, and hopped to freedom, where

he likely continues to breed like a bunny, sending his little offspring to harass the big, brooding guy with the bad karma.

5
Hair Today, Gone Tomorrow

Wisconsin author Michael Perry once had long locks. He keeps his hair shorn short these days. In speeches, he blames it on "generalized crop failure."

In the audience, I nod knowingly.

I've had a hairy face since high school. It started with sideburns, though looking back, that "style" seems ghastly. Then my varsity basketball coach suggested my mustache made me a marked man in the conference.

So be it, I figured. It was his way of hinting that a shave was in order. I wasn't going there.

My facial forest has always been furiously feral. My 5 o'clock shadow shows up shortly after lunch.

I grew a goatee before graduating from high school, and I've had facial hair every year since. I shaved my beard once, when my son, Josh, was just two. Thinking that suddenly emerging from the bathroom sans furry face might scare him, I sat him on the stool to watch me shave.

I cleared one side first, stopped and asked his assessment.

He gazed up at me and said, "Put it back on."

Too late for that. It all came off, but I let it regrow months later.

My mother always wondered how the hair atop my head could be brown while the fuzz on my chin grew black.

She need not wonder any longer. The facial hair has turned a rich gray that makes me look older than my age. But that isn't the only cruel trick nature is pulling.

The hairline, like that of many men my age, is receding rapidly. I sweep my hair up and back daily using a comb with wide teeth so as not to permanently dislodge yet another single strand from a failing follicle. Dabbing on sculpting lotion to settle what remains, I shudder at the thought of an eventual comb-over.

Each day, on my first trip to the bathroom, I glance in the mirror and, sure enough, some wild hair is sticking straight out, ridiculously perpendicular from my head.

"Why resist behaving when so few of you remain?" I'll say to that mug in the mirror.

Worse, gaze closely, and I discover things are changing all over my face. A lone hair grows wild on my nose, though far above the nostrils, and another has sprouted on my cheek just along the left side of my nose. Pluck them, and they sprout again.

Why grow there? Why not join the thinning crowd atop my scalp? Heck, they could help me skip wearing hats to avoid the risk of sunburn.

Speaking of nostrils, the hair in there insists on growing as wild as a wheat field. Trimming is a nearly weekly necessity, lest I frighten passersby.

Likewise, my eyebrows have always been hideously gnarly, as if some microscopic gardener keeps tossing down more fertilizer. Actually, "they" always were more of an "it"—the dreaded unibrow. Thankfully, the patch above my nose has thinned, though a single white strand grows ridiculously long and requires clipping.

The stretch above each eye continues restless, its rampant growth unruly. Too often, brow hairs dangle down and poke and prod my eyelids. They even scratch my glasses. I find myself smoothing out my brows each morning so devilish little hair horns aren't pointing skyward.

My hairstylist trims these without extra charge. Sometimes, in between such visits, I take a scissors to them.

Watch some silly dating show, and you'll hear women say again and again that they're not interested in bald guys.

But I look at my uncles and figure, in a few years, yep, that's me. Even stepson Adam is quick to point out the growing bald spot on the backside of my head.

Meanwhile, the hair on the back of my neck grows like a tangle of tumbleweeds.

It's just another cruel joke from Mother Nature.

Perhaps, however, if I stop taking the clippers to those neckline clumps, some day they just might help with that comb-over.

6
Remembering Our Sweet Little Travel Companion

My wife, Cheryl, and I once had a great travel mate, a female friend who never had to stop for a potty break. She never got hungry, never wasted money on souvenirs, and never whined nor asked "Are we there yet?"

When Cheryl and I weren't traveling, this friend stayed with us. She became part of the family. And she never raided our refrigerator.

We dubbed her Ms. Garmin.

In the days before we carried phones in our pockets, Ms. Garmin was our constant companion when we hit the open road. Almost always, she was a great help, especially when we rolled down unfamiliar highways.

"Drive 32 miles on Interstate 90," she told us in South Dakota. "In point nine miles, turn right on South Dakota Highway BB. Turn right on South Dakota Highway BB."

With Ms. Garmin along, stuck on the inside of the windshield like some large, inverted bug, we could tell at a glance our estimated time of arrival and whether we'd entered a reduced-speed zone without easing off the cruise control.

At times, however, Ms. Garmin tested our patience.

For example, she might say, "In point four miles, keep right on U.S. 84, then turn right on Debbie Downer Road." As we approached the turn and before she could catch her breath, she'd say, "Keep right on U.S. 84, then turn right on Debbie Downer Road," followed by, "Turn right on Debbie Downer Road."

"Alright, already," I'd reply. "Can you wait until we reach the dang corner?"

Ms. Garmin also could be a slow starter some mornings, as if we needed to dump a cup of coffee on her. Sometimes her mind seemed in a fog as her indicators suggested she searched for a satellite.

"Heck, it's not foggy, and we're not passing skyscrapers. What's the problem?" I said in frustration.

Finally, she came around.

She had another habit even more irritating.

"Recalculating," she said with slight sarcasm whenever I missed her commanded turn.

That was particularly annoying when we visited a state such as Vermont and the next colorful hillside, rustic barn, or waterfall was just around the corner, enticing me to pull over, whip a U-turn, and grab a photo.

"Recalculating," Ms. Garmin said snidely, and I wished the geniuses who created her had included a "photo-op" pause button on her technologically advanced brain.

The worst part was that Ms. Garmin could be so reliable so often that we began to depend on her, and then she let us down, disappointing us like some wayward child.

For example, Cheryl and I were returning from Maryland and had just hit a ramp to the freeway back toward Wisconsin.

"In point four miles, turn right on Hornybrook Road."

"What? You want us to drive into that field?"

Ms. Garmin seemed to be getting even for all those missed turns.

Another time, we were zigzagging through a small river town in Maine, and Ms. Garmin turned us down a dead-end road that wound past several paper mills.

But Cheryl and I haven't forgotten the time we were leaving San Francisco, on our way to Yosemite National Park. It was one of those early-morning drives, and Ms. Garmin, perhaps a tad sleepy, said, "In point four miles, turn right on County A."

"There's no County A in San Francisco," I told Cheryl.

Apparently, Ms. Garmin didn't like that. Soon after, we were rolling across the 4.5-mile Bay Bridge, and she ordered, "In point nine miles, turn right on County A."

"What are you talking about?"

"In point four miles, turn right on County A."

"No way, unless you expect us to take a chilly early-morning swim with the sharks."

7
A Snake Beside the Frozen Steaks

One summer in Marshall, while I was home from college, I put a snake in my parents' freezer.

Don't fret; it was already dead.

I acquired the snake in August 1978, when my Uncle Louie Klecker's hired hand, Mike Wells, and I were returning from a day of haying at the Phil Mess farm. Mike was driving Louie's light blue Chevy pickup as we took Medina Road toward Tower Line Road, which connected to Box Elder Road, where Louie lived.

With the windows rolled down on that hot summer day, alfalfa chaff and the smell of sweat swirled around us. We spotted something long lying in the road ahead of us, and Mike stomped on the brakes, but it was too late.

"Holy, crap," I said, though I actually used a word more likely uttered when one steps in a cowpie. "Did you see that?" I pivoted and gazed out the back window. "Was it a rattler?"

"I don't think so," Mike said. "Probably a bullsnake."

"A what?"

I'd never seen a bullsnake and shuddered at my considerable risk of coming in contact with one while strolling through a hayfield or almost anywhere on a southern Wisconsin dairy farm. Had I spotted one at Louie's, I would have screamed and scrambled for shelter, probably running until I reached his aging farmhouse.

Mike whipped a U-turn. Hopping out, we examined the beast, which, like so many raccoons and rabbits and rodents that risk life and limb on rural roads, didn't make it across.

"Man, that thing is awesome," I said, hesitant to get too close, even with a hayfork I pulled from the pickup. I poked it. "Is it poisonous?"

"Naw," Mike said. He grabbed the fork from me and scooped it up. "They're actually good because they eat mice and rats and gophers."

Bullsnakes, as my parents' Encyclopedia Britannica later told me, are considered a subspecies of the gopher snake. They generally range from four to six feet long but can grow to more than eight feet.

They also can be intimidating when threatened and, instead of relying on venom, use constriction to kill their prey.

I wondered how big their prey could be.

Regardless, this one was dead—the truck tire caught and mangled its head. Mike tossed it in the pickup box, and we proceeded back to Louie's.

This bullsnake was already dead. It might have looked menacing had it not been for its mangled head, which my brother Tom was holding up with a clear piece of fishing line as I snapped this photo.

At day's end, I shoved the reptile in a gunnysack, tossed the sack in my car trunk and drove home. I curled the snake in a plastic trash bag and put it in our basement freezer, a bin so long I could have laid down in it.

Mom, cooking supper, came over to see what I was up to but stopped dead when she saw the snake.

"What are you doing with that?" she cried.

"Freezing it," I replied, irritated because my intent seemed obvious. Somehow, I thought that, having dealt with the shenanigans of three sons, she would be okay with it. I guessed wrong, but the snake stayed in the freezer anyhow.

I was three years out of high school and from time to time invited friends over for small parties in our basement rec room. At one party, after each of us had downed a couple of beers, I moseyed over to the freezer, flipped open the lid, whipped out the stiffly curled snake and proclaimed, "Look!"

It freaked out the girls, and even some of the guys. But because the number of young ladies interested in coming to my parties was limited, the gag soon got old.

Eventually, I disposed of the snake, and Mom breathed a sigh of relief. Whether I pitched it in the trash or gave it a solemn burial in the backyard, I cannot recall.

But more than forty years later, I remembered I had a black and white Polaroid of younger brother Tom holding up that snake, soon after the kill. Tom and I had a contentious relationship in his early years because he often played with and broke my model cars and other prized possessions, but in adulthood we developed a brotherly respect sprinkled with the occasional jab of humor.

I dug through one box of files, then another before finding the picture tucked in an envelope amid birthday and baptismal scenes. There stood Tom, a skinny kid with a dish-bowl cut of dark hair, huge spectacles turning dark as sunglasses with the outdoor light, tee shirt with pocket, ridiculously short shorts of the era and equally ridiculous high sweat socks under what looked like track shoes—though I'm certain he never ran track—holding the tail of the bullsnake head high. The snake's head still reached the pavement in front of the closed garage door. I don't know how tall Tom was back then, but he certainly stood four feet or better.

I'd forgotten about a second photo, which showed the snake's body in an S curl. Tom, out of the picture, held its head up with an invisible strand of monofilament fishing line so the snake would look menacing. It might have except for that badly squished end with the fangs.

This being the era of instant electronic communications, I whipped out my cell phone and asked Tom how old he was in August 1978 (schooled a journalist, I never was strong at math; it was quicker to have Tom do the figuring).

"Thirteen," came his quick reply.

My brother Tom, then 13, held up the dead bullsnake in a 1978 photo.

I used my phone to snap a photo of the photo showing Tom and texted it back to him.

"That's the snake you brought home," he said.

"Yup," I replied. "On the left, you mean."

8
Nuts, Just Minimum Wage

Each year, hundreds of black walnuts fell annually from a handful of trees on property Cheryl and I owned on the Wisconsin River across from Muscoda.

Year-round homes sandwiched our large lot on Effigy Mounds Road, and mature trees filled much of the sloped land. Every month or so, I drove there to mow, fish, and pitch my tent for a couple of days. That was my plan in September 1999.

The black walnuts had already fallen. Grinding them up would be hard on the mower, but a weekly state Department of Natural Resources report said DNR offices were buying walnuts for its nurseries at $3 a bushel.

So I started picking and counting. With 300 in my lawn cart, I guessed they'd fill a bushel basket. When I hit 900, or three bushels worth, the cart was so heavy I couldn't wrestle it into my pickup truck without dumping some out. I switched containers and filled three large garbage bags.

After two hours of toil, I had amassed at least seven bushels, enough to pay for a run the 16 miles to a DNR office in Boscobel. Besides, I'd be benefiting the environment, nurturing nature, and propagating this tree species.

When I arrived, a female worker greeted me at a service counter.

"I understand you're buying black walnuts," I said.

"Sorry," she said. "Those came in early this year. We've already bought what we need."

Chagrined, I said, "I drove all the way here from Muscoda. What am I gonna do with half a pickup load of walnuts?"

"Well, I noticed a sign between here and Muscoda that said 'Walnuts wanted.' Why not watch for it on your way back and stop there?"

"Thanks," I said. "I'll do that."

But when I passed the halfway point of Blue River without seeing the sign, my optimism faded. This person probably had his fill, as well, I thought.

As I neared Muscoda, however, I spotted the sign.

Walnuts were more plentiful on our river lot than area buyers.

"How many walnuts are you looking to buy?" I asked a woman who answered my knock.

"All you can give me," she said, much to my relief.

This Mennonite family had a husking machine and was buying nuts for an out-of-state processor. The woman sent her son out to work the husker, and together we loaded the machine. The kid, perhaps still in his teens, seemed a tad slow-witted.

The husked nuts filled two large bags.

"You'll have to ask my mom how much they're worth," he said. "She's better at figuring that stuff than me."

The mother came out to weigh them. "You've got 88 pounds here," she said, "and we're paying 10 cents a pound."

My grand total, for two hours of hard labor plus my gas and time driving round-trip to Boscobel, was $8.80.

The next fall, the walnuts went under the mower. Sharpening the blade afterward was less work than bending and picking.

9
"This Is Only a Test"

"You folks are magicians," I told the nurse doting over me.

"Why do you say that?"

"Who else could prod patients into voluntarily abusing their bodies so profoundly in preparation for the abuse yet to come?"

Fortunately, the test I was about to undergo is required only once a decade for folks older than 50. That's assuming, of course, that your test turns out as clean as, ahem, a whistle.

I'm talking about a colonoscopy.

For those of you who've never had the, um, pleasure, let me offer insight. A colonoscopy is an endoscopic exam of the large colon and part of the small bowel with a fiber optic camera on a flexible tube passed through the anus.

I wondered what kind of doctor desires to do this to strangers and friends alike.

My family physician set me up with Doctor William Brandt at Janesville's Dean Riverview Clinic. Brandt explained the extensive preparations and said he used Golytely to clean the bowels because it was the most thorough option available.

He'd get no argument there.

He also said it was safer than using sodium phosphate enemas, which can cause kidney failure and other nasty stuff, including death.

Okay, he sold me on Golytcly. His office called in the prescription for the preparation kit to the Walgreens next to my athletic club. I had two weeks before my colonoscopy. I planned to pick up the kit the next time I worked out. Walgreens left a phone message saying my kit was ready. A day later, the store's automated caller dialed me again and said, "Please pick it up within 24 hours or it will be put back on the shelf."

Geez, alright already; threaten me and I'll forget the whole thing.

I wanted my appointment on a Tuesday—my workday with the most flexibility. I worked at *The Janesville Gazette* and scheduled the exam for 11:30 a.m. I figured to do enough preparations for the next day's paper before seeing Brandt so I wouldn't have to go back.

Foolish move. I wasn't thinking about the morning-long hunger.

The week before my test, Brandt's nurse called to ask if I understood the directions.

"Yes, but I like to eat."

"Oh, you can eat lots of things," she said, listing soda pop, Jello, fruit juices, and chicken and beef broth.

"You don't understand," I said. "I like to *eat*."

Two days before my test, between 6 and 8 p.m., I had to drink a 10-ounce bottle of magnesium citrate. I was up and down half the night and figured by morning that I must be cleaned out. But no, I had more than 24 hours left to go.

That Monday, I was limited to clear liquids—as long as they weren't red, a color the doctor might mistake for blood.

I went through a Campbell's can of chicken broth and another of beef. Trust me, one can of each is plenty for one day. There's a reason people prefer soup with chunks of meat and veggies.

I ate Jello and downed soda, green tea, and white grape juice.

At work, a nearby reporter was doing a phone interview about Girl Scout cookies. I wanted to toss an empty Coke can at her.

About 5 p.m., just minutes after sipping my last bowl of broth, I started downing my gallon jug of Golytely. The directions told me to aim for a 10-ounce glass every 10 to 15 minutes but to slow down in case of nausea or vomiting. Fortunately, the directions also suggested mixing in Crystal Light—again, any color but red. Without the sweetener, I wouldn't have kept the Golytely down.

Not that it hung around long anyhow, if you get my drift.

When I emerged from the bathroom, my wife asked for an update, and I gave her the gory details while hoping to stop downing the dreaded fluid.

"Keep drinking," she said.

"Thanks for the support."

All night, the toilet became my best friend. Sleep was just a dream.

By the time I finished work and made it to Brandt's office, my fatigue and growling stomach had me on edge, to put it politely.

I stripped down and donned a surgical gown as directed before sitting in a recliner behind a curtain in a tiny waiting cubby hole. A nurse gave me a cozy heated blanket that took the chill out of the air, and she asked if I wanted anything to read.

"No. I've barely slept for two nights. I'll just catch a few winks."

"Okay," she said. "I'll flip the light off then."

"Just don't forget about me."

I drifted off and awakened overhearing my name. It seemed like I'd been there for hours. Let's get on with it, I thought.

Soon another nurse led me to what she politely called the "procedure" room.

"What a nice, sanitized name," I said.

I lay down on a surgery table. The room was cool, and the nurse asked if I wanted a second heated blanket.

"No thanks," I said, assuming it would add to my bill.

Twenty minutes passed, and I tucked my chilled feet under the now-cooled blanket but away from the chilly metal footrest that probably keeps patients from sliding off the table during the "procedure."

The nurse popped in again. "Let me get you another blanket."

"How much will this cost?"

"Oh, we don't charge for each individual item," she said as she tossed it atop me. "It's one lump sum no matter what we use."

I was surprised.

Gazing at a nearby TV monitor, I guessed it probably wasn't for watching "SportsCenter." The room seemed unnecessarily large. It had two chairs on the far side. When Doc Brandt finally arrived, I asked, "Those chairs over there, are those for spectators?"

Brandt said they're for family members who want to be with a patient until the "procedure" starts. Then he shoos them out in case "complications" arise.

He explained possible risks to the "procedure" but said trouble only arises in about one in 600 patients.

"So, I'm pretty safe."

"Oh yes," he said. "The last 599 patients turned out just fine."

I chuckled. Brandt started an IV medicine drip to knock me out. I didn't have time to ask him why anyone would go through many years of expensive schooling only to spend workdays gazing up people's back sides.

The next thing I knew, Brandt was hovering over me, telling me my test came out clear. I remember that but don't recall getting dressed.

The staff gave me a snack to take the edge off my empty stomach, but I don't remember what. Two days later, I found my patient wrist ID band in my coat pocket. I also don't recall putting it there.

I was just grateful that patient No. 600 came out fine, too.

10
How I Wed on My Birthday

Cheryl and I were engaged but hadn't set a wedding date when we decided to take a May 1998 trip to Hawaii.

"Maybe we should get married while we're there," I suggested. "It would be romantic."

"Maybe so," she agreed.

Cheryl was overseeing vacation planning, although the four-island venture was part of a guided trip through Trieloff Tours out of Baltimore.

"Which island would you like to get married on?" she asked.

"Makes no difference to me, whichever you want."

"I'd like to get married on Maui, but there's one problem," she said.

"What's that?"

"The only day we have a break from sightseeing there is your birthday. You don't want to get married on your birthday, do you?"

"Well, if we do, I'll never forget our anniversary."

We were both raised Catholic and had gone through divorces and the church's annulment process. However, after we learned the church would still require us to attend marriage preparation programs, which we had no time to take, Cheryl hired a wedding planner. The planner lined up a nondenominational minister, a photographer, and a ceremony site—a cute white gazebo at a seaside hotel next door to our tour's hotel, outside of historic Lahaina.

We left for Hawaii on an early-morning bus from Janesville to Chicago's O'Hare International Airport. As we were about to pull out, one of two older ladies sitting together a few rows ahead of us ambled back to say hello. She introduced herself as Lorraine Jacques.

Lorraine Jacques, left, and Catherine Grebe were best friends who lived across the street from each other in Janesville. We didn't know them when we left for Hawaii, but by the time we got married on Maui, they became our unofficial "bridesmaids."

"Are you the two getting married on this tour?" she asked enthusiastically.

"Yes," I replied. "On Maui, on the 12th, which is my birthday."

"Great!" Lorraine said. "We heard about your plan from the travel agent, and we're so excited about it."

"That's nice," Cheryl said, and Lorraine returned to her seat.

Cheryl turned to me. "You be careful; those two look like trouble."

I wondered what she meant.

Before we reached the big island of Hawaii, Lorraine, traveling with her neighbor across the street, Catherine Grebe, talked the plane's crew out of a bottle of champagne to share with us on our wedding day.

Cheryl and I enjoy a champagne toast after we said our marriage vows on my birthday in a gazebo on the island of Maui.

Maui was the third island on our tour, and by the time we reached it Lorraine and Catherine, both widows, had become our friends. Contrary to Cheryl's concern, they were no trouble at all. In fact, just the opposite. Lorraine liked to tip a drink or two and even wore a Hawaiian lei around her neck. But this one wasn't your typical lei featuring flowers; it was a plastic mesh sleeve filled with miniature liquor bottles. Catherine, in contrast, didn't drink a drop, but sometimes you wouldn't know it. She could be as much fun as Lorraine.

I'll never forget the night Lorraine joined us for a drink at a poolside table outside our hotel after a day of touring.

"Where's Catherine?" we asked.

"Oh, she's getting ready for bed already."

Cheryl and I looked at each other and simultaneously started chanting: "Catherine? Catherine? Can Catherine come out to play?"

Catherine leaned over her second-floor balcony. "I would, but I already have my hair in rollers."

"So what?" I said. "We don't care, and no one else here knows you. Come on down!"

She did. That's the way she was.

When we finished sightseeing the day before our ceremony, we had to apply for a marriage license. The county clerk told us to meet her not at the courthouse but at her house during an appointed evening time slot.

Lorraine, left, and Catherine helped us mark an anniversary with a meal at the Olive Garden in Janesville.

"Don't be early, and don't be late," she warned.

We called a cab, and a young driver arrived. I told him the address, and he said, "I don't know where that is."

My stomach surged with anxiety. "Well, you'd better figure it out in a hurry," I said.

Fortunately, he did figure it out. We arrived on time at the clerk's home, in a crowded residential neighborhood, and signed the necessary paperwork.

Catherine and Lorraine planned to join us at our wedding, and several other couples asked if they could come, as well.

"The more the merrier," we said.

As Cheryl and I said our "I do's," Catherine and Lorraine served as our unofficial "bridesmaids."

It started to sprinkle as the ceremony ended.

"Hawaiians believe a light rain, descending from the mountains, is good luck at a wedding," the minister told us.

We smiled and later, under sunny skies, strolled along the beach for photographs.

Then we went up to Catherine and Lorraine's room to pop the champagne and share a wedding cake these creative women crafted from doughnuts. Laughs filled our celebration.

Getting that aforementioned marriage license wasn't so funny, however. Cheryl and I returned home, but the document that would make our marriage official still hadn't arrived weeks later when we drove up to Minocqua to see my parents. Mom had invited her brother Fran and his wife, Judy, for supper. As we sat down to eat, Mom blurted out, "So, are you two married, or not?"

Knowing what a stickler for Catholic doctrine my Aunt Judy is, I nearly fell out of my chair. I feared she might have a coronary.

Eventually, the marriage license came. Cheryl and I had, indeed, gotten married in Hawaii, and true to my word, I have never forgotten our anniversary. From time to time through the years, we've even celebrated with our pair of wonderfully wacky "bridesmaids."

11
Fear? Not!

She's trained them well,
their mother has.
If a creepy crawls,
they'll scamper and scoot.
Should a bee or fly
or skeeter draw near,
they'll duck and dodge
and dart for the door.
"Eek! A spider!
"Help, Papa!" they'll
plead to their grandpa.
"I nearly died
"from that black widow,"
their mother justifies.
An arachnophobe, as a result.
And reasonable? Sure.
But she fans childhood fears
into near paranoia.
Ah, but Papa got the last laugh.
He took the oldest
on a boat when she
was barely past diapers.
He taught her to fetch
a worm or even—
Don't look Mom!—a leach.

This granddaughter did so
and still fears not today.
She even caressed the critter,
before her Papa
impaled it on a fish hook
and tossed it overboard.

12
Sad Saga of a Sagging Sofa

Cheryl, who suffers with back problems, suggested our soft, sagging sofa might be to blame and was sold on buying a new, firmer model.

Trying to be a loving husband, I agreed.

We found one at our favorite Madison furniture store. The price, including sales tax, $100 for delivery and a two-year insurance plan offering free replacement for any damage, was a staggering $1,400.

Normally I'd scoff at insurance as a retailing scam to extract more dough out of softie customers, but I had visions of our 2-year-old grandson, the Kid of Perpetual Motion, dumping his grape juice on the sofa on his next visit after being told to keep the juice in the kitchen.

We had a few weeks before delivery, so our next move was to get rid of our sadly sagging sofa, off-white with patches of blue and mauve—not pink. No problem, I figured. I'd photograph it and place a free ad in the newspaper where I worked. I could get it gone during my furlough without having to deal with it during a workweek.

Cheryl and I settled on a price of $140. I waited eagerly by the phone that didn't ring.

After we dropped the price to $90, an older gentleman called. He'd hurry right over. Well, he hurried as much as he could. This elderly fellow could barely walk up the driveway. After sitting on our sofa, he struggled to get up and suggested it lacked sufficient support.

Still, he said, his grandson would be over that weekend, and if we still had it, maybe he'd come and get it.

We still had it, all right, so I called. He said he'd come when his grandson arrived.

Later, he called and said, "Sorry, I just don't think it's right for me."

The phone stayed silent. The 10-day ad ran out, and so did my furlough.

Having failed my foray into furniture sales, I was glad to be employed as a journalist.

Plan B was giving the sofa to charity. But we had to hurry because the new sofa, with its firm foundation, already graced our living room. The sagging sofa now filled my half of the garage. My car sat out in the early spring elements.

I wasn't sure Goodwill took couches, so I called Acts of Kindness. The charity's founder, Shelly, said sure, they take sofas. "How about if I contact someone who needs one, and that person can arrange to pick it up?"

"Okay," I said with a feeling of misgivings.

A woman called that afternoon. She seemed excited as I described it. She agreed to call later to arrange a pickup time.

She never called back.

I called Shelly after another frustrating morning of scraping frost off my windshield because, well, that dang sofa was parked in the garage.

"I'll find someone else," Shelly assured me.

A guy soon called and agreed to pick it up at noon Friday.

Later that day, "Heather" left a message. "I hope you still have that sofa because we'd love it. We ran into real tough times and lost everything, even our beds. A sofa would be lovely."

I called and told Heather that someone else was coming to get it. "If he doesn't show up, I'll call you."

At about 12:15 that Friday, the guy called and said he couldn't find a friend with a truck.

"Where do you live?" I asked.

"Beloit."

That was 10 miles away, and I wasn't about to deliver it.

I left a message with Heather.

Cheryl and I planned to spend Saturday night in New Glarus, but I first had to shovel an inch of heavy snow off the driveway.

We hopped in my vehicle, which was sitting in the driveway, of course, and I turned on the wipers to clear the snow. It was so heavy, the wipers stopped on the upswing.

I got out and pushed off the snow, and the wipers returned to their down position.

We headed across town, and slush from passing cars splashed my vehicle. I hit the wipers, and the blades got hooked together. I stopped and got out. "This wouldn't have happened if we didn't have that darn sofa in the garage," I snorted.

"It wouldn't have happened if you hadn't been too lazy to brush off the snow," Cheryl retorted.

The entanglement wrecked the wiper blades. Worse, one arm appeared bent.

"We can't drive to New Glarus without wipers," I said.

Returning home, we got Cheryl's car and arrived in New Glarus later than planned.

When we got home Sunday, I found a message from Heather. "I got a friend's truck, and we want to pick up the sofa today."

"Today" being Saturday, of course.

I called back and left a message. "Sorry, we weren't home Saturday. Stop and pick it up today."

Being no mechanical genius, I called a buddy about the wiper problem. He stopped over and determined that the one arm was naturally bent, and that a loose bolt caused the entanglement.

I bought new wiper blades, the best available, at an auto parts store for $41 and change.

Heather didn't come or call. I left her a message Monday. "Come and get it any night this week."

Each day, I grew more frustrated while scraping overnight frost from windows. Another week went by. Heather never called back.

By the next Wednesday, Cheryl had heard enough whining. She called several charities and compiled the options.

I called one, and they could pick it up Tuesday. "Oh, I was hoping to get it out of the garage this week. What time Tuesday?"

"We can't guarantee a time; between 8 and noon."

"What if it rains?" I said. "I'd better watch the forecast."

Heck, I knew if I placed the couch at the curb with a "free" sign, it would vanish in short order. This being spring in Wisconsin, however, who could guarantee a dry day? I didn't want the sagging-but-still-usable sofa to wind up a soaking, unusable hulk.

Cheryl had called Goodwill, but no one answered. I, too, got no answer—not even a message machine—that evening. While Cheryl cooked supper, I stewed and got out my tape measure.

I determined I could squeeze the sofa into my small SUV, even if it meant leaving the back door, which swung to the side instead of up, hanging open. We could take the sofa to Goodwill if they accepted sofas.

"Let's drive to Goodwill," I said after supper.

A Goodwill employee unloading a carload of stuff said, "Yes, we take sofas."

Cheryl and I drove back home, muscled the big-but-sagging sofa into my little SUV, attached a red flag on the back as if we were hauling lumber, and returned to Goodwill.

Finally, the sagging sofa was gone.

I'm surprised it didn't fall out the back of my vehicle. That it didn't start pouring. And that my SUV's back door still closed without the hinges getting bent from driving with the door hanging open.

I was just glad the sofa was history. Heck, instead of selling it to help offset the cost of the new couch, the sagging sofa cost me only $41 and a few weeks of frustration.

Give away a couch? Nothing to it.

13
Rental Car Recoil

In May 2010, Cheryl and I flew hundreds of miles for a two-week vacation in Seattle, Portland, and Vancouver. We had pored over tourism brochures and picked out sightseeing spots. We booked hotels, plotted travel routes, and noted can't-miss restaurants. We were confident in our planning.

At an Enterprise rental counter near the Sea-Tac Airport in Seattle, I saved a few bucks by picking a low-cost Chevrolet Cobalt, then reluctantly agreed to spend almost $200 more for a GPS unit to help navigate strange streets. However, then the agent asked if we wanted to invest nearly $200 more for insurance.

I hesitated, glancing out the window to where Cheryl stood guard over our luggage.

"Um, I think my auto insurance covers us," I replied, uncertain because I hadn't rented a car since the 1994 Rose Bowl. "So, no thank you."

I walked out, paperwork in one hand and key fob in the other, doubt filling my mind.

"I didn't know whether to insure the rental," I told Cheryl.

"So why didn't you?"

"Because I think our auto insurance covers us. Besides, I'd already agreed to the GPS unit. How much more can we afford? I think I've read that rental insurance deals are rip-offs. Besides, what could go wrong?"

I feared regretting those words as an attendant pulled up with our gleaming little red Chevy. He urged us to inspect it for flaws. I pointed out dings and scratches, and he dutifully noted them.

47

We reached our Seattle hotel with ease. We pulled the GPS unit off the dashboard so no one would consider breaking in to swipe it. We spent the day sightseeing on foot. Early the next morning, Cheryl noticed a chip in the windshield—right where the GPS unit had obscured it from view.

"Did you point that out to the rental place?" she asked.

"No. I didn't see it. Maybe we can call Enterprise later and let them know about it. Maybe they'll let it slide."

We sped off to join a whale watching tour. A chip was no big deal, we reasoned. We had owned cars with windshield chips, and they never caused problems.

As we drove north to catch a ferry at a seaside village, the GPS unit kept sputtering. The cord seemed to have a short, which didn't help us find the ferry dock. By the time we located it, the captain was sounding his ship's horn. We frantically tried to buy a parking pass at a self-serve kiosk, but the unfamiliar gadget wouldn't work. We figured we'd deal with payment later, hurried to the office to buy ferry tickets, and ran up the ramp as the boat's engines roared to life and attendants started to pull the walkway. I felt like O.J. Simpson running through an airport in that famous commercial. Just as the ferry started moving, we leaped aboard—the last passengers.

We later boarded a tour boat, and calling Enterprise became an afterthought as we spent all day without spotting a whale.

The next day, on the road to Mount St. Helen's, we again thought to call Enterprise, but Cheryl couldn't get a cell phone connection. One morning later, I was wishing we had taken the insurance policy as I drove the treacherous, snow-covered ridges of Mount Hood, where we hoped to eat breakfast at famous Timberline Lodge.

Screaming squad cars passed us—heading to some crash on the slick highway, I imagined. Soon, we were gingerly winding up a road leading to the lodge. In the parking lot, we stepped out in sneakers into snow six inches deep as skiers glided past.

"Maybe we should skip breakfast, quickly tour the lodge, and leave before the snow gets worse," I reasoned as flakes fell heavily.

"I think you're right," Cheryl said.

We climbed in the car fifty minutes later, and I flipped on the heater and defroster. A mile down the mountainside, we heard a loud pop and the windshield suddenly sported a horizontal three-foot crack emanating from our seemingly innocent little chip. We made it off the mountain without sliding into the wild white yonder. We called the rental company as soon as we reached our hotel.

"You should have called as soon as you noticed the chip," a female agent told me.

"I know," I said. "But we're on vacation. Whenever we thought about it, we couldn't get cell phone service."

"I'll mark it down, but I can't guarantee anything."

We visited Vancouver a few days later, and at 8 a.m. drove to 1,000-acre Stanley Park. We stopped to observe world-famous totem poles as hundreds of race runners clogged a path that circled the park. We walked over a knoll, less than 100 yards from the parking lot, when a horn started beeping.

"Is that our car?" Cheryl asked.

"I don't know, but why would it be?"

I pulled the key fob from my pocket, and, as we headed toward the lot, the honking stopped. A woman was calmly getting out of one of just three parked cars. Nothing seemed amiss.

We headed for our next stop, where a picturesque lighthouse diverts ships from the island's rocky shore. That's when I realized my door handle was ajar and I spotted a gouge in the paint below the lock. Someone had tried breaking in! We felt fortunate that the person failed because Cheryl had left her purse on the floor, under her jacket. We checked the trunk, and our suitcases were still with us.

"Wow," I said. "First the windshield; now this. We might be on the hook for 1,000 bucks."

"We should call the police," Cheryl suggested.

"What would Canadian authorities do for us? Track down the perp?" I said, using lingo from a favorite TV crime show. "Hold up our vacation? Let's just keep going."

Back in Seattle three days later, I pulled in to Enterprise, where I explained the windshield crack as an attendant made notes and nodded.

"Seems you have a problem with the door handle," he said. "Did someone try breaking in?"

"We think so." I explained what happened.

Inside, I filled out paperwork to expedite repairs. A male clerk made a print of my credit card to assure payment.

"We'll need a phone number to get in touch after we get an estimate," he said.

As we flew home, I hoped the windshield of our plane had no chips.

A week passed before we got a bill of $433.15 to repair the door lock, handle, and paint gouge. Included were costs for the car being out of service two days while work was done. We skated by without paying for a new windshield.

Our insurer paid the bill, minus a $250 deductible I had to cover.

That wasn't the end of it. I recalled the ordeal for a buddy who said, "Wait a minute, did you pay for the rental with a credit card? If so, the credit card might cover that cost."

Indeed, we had. That led to more phone calls and more paperwork. That quest, however, ended in a conversation with an agent.

"Sorry, we cover collisions, but not vandalism," he said.

"So, what you're saying is, had we totaled the car, we'd have been covered?"

"Correct."

14
Just Like Animals

They trekked and traveled
from near and far.
Their mission focused, frantic, fearless.
Their aim: To defile and destroy,
To plunder and pillage
Their ill-gotten goods.
They clambered, climbed, and clawed,
And in the atrocious aftermath,
Their devastating destruction
Proved obvious, painful.
Feeling saucy and sassy,
Privileged and permitted,
They ransacked and raided.
They shredded property
And stole provisions.
They tore horrible holes,
Creating chaos while
Feeling exempted and entitled.
Until the thugs and troublemakers,
These beasts and brutes,
Were captured and collared,
To be led away one and all,
Crying over being caged,
like the animals they were.
In the end, a higher authority
Took control and triumphed,
Sparking rejoicing and revelry.

While these pirates and perpetrators,
These outlaws and offenders,
May reemerge and return
To the scene of their crime
To hang around and haunt again,
Authorities wielding power
Who hauled them away hope
These damn squirrels learned a lesson
And leave the bird feeders for the birds!

15
A Granddaughter's Worldly Wisdom

In the 1950s and 1960s, Art Linkletter hosted a radio show with a segment dubbed, "Kids Say the Darndest Things." Judging from what I hear from kids in my own family, that could still prove popular today.

When my son, Josh, was age two, I decided to shave off my beard. So he wouldn't be startled at suddenly seeing a clean-shaven guy who looked somewhat like Dad, I sat him on the toilet seat so he could watch while I shaved.

I trimmed off one side first, then turned.

"Josh, how do I look?"

"Put it back on."

I took him to church at that age, as well. We sat in the "crying room" in case he acted up. Before the service, the priest passed behind us. Josh, standing up in the pew and looking back, spotted him.

"Hi, God!" he blurted.

Those days did little to prepare me for spending a summer week with my granddaughter when Lexi was eight. I don't recall Josh being as worldly at that age as Lexi was.

I took Lexi up north for a few days of fishing. As we started out, she spotted a bicyclist riding on the road's narrow shoulder.

"Papa, he needs really good balance or he'll wind up being ground meat," she said.

With Lexi seated beside me, we passed the time on the long drive by playing games. We chewed gum, and though it wasn't bubble gum, we had a contest to see who could blow bubbles the fastest. Lexi claimed to have popped one, but I said I didn't hear it so it didn't count.

"Bubbles can have no sound," she reasoned. "Just like farts."

When we switched to finding recognizable figures among the clouds, I said, "Look, there's a toilet seat."

"That's so wrong!" she said.

After arriving, we soon went bluegill fishing. When we needed to dig another white wax worm out of the bait box, one was dying and had turned brown.

"Use that one," Lexi said. "It's a limited edition."

On our drive home, Lexi told of touring the Egyptian exhibit during a school trip to Chicago's Field Museum of Natural History. She suggested the exhibit was "inappropriate."

"Why's that?" I asked.

"Because there were these two Egyptian dudes, Papa, and one dude had underwear and the other guy didn't. You could see his nuts. It was awesome."

"I thought you said it was inappropriate."

Explained Lexi, "Oh, that's only if you were a parent."

16
Coming to Blows with a Snowblower

It was May 18—well into spring—when I asked my wife to help carry our snowblower into the basement. It wasn't for storage, mind you, but because the two rubber rotor blades needed replacing.

"Why are you doing this now?" Cheryl asked. "We're not expecting snow anytime soon."

"That's exactly why I'm doing it now. I have the time, and I don't want to wait until a snowstorm is barreling toward us."

Placing the Toro snowthrower on my heavy-duty work table, I figured, would make the job easier. If I sat on a stool, the paddle housing would be at eye level.

I'd already put off this project for months, reminded every time I stepped into my workshop by the pungent smell of fresh rubber in the shipping box I'd already opened. This wasn't the first time I tackled the task. I didn't recall the details, but I did remember that this wasn't a simple chore.

Just after lunch, I dug out the instruction manual and reviewed the section on paddle replacement. It seemed simple enough. Loosen a bolt securing the rotor halves to the rotor shaft and remove two more holding the center of each blade. Then remove the two torx screws and locknuts holding each end of each blade.

That's when the trouble began. I had a torx hex key set with seven different sizes that folded out like jackknife blades. There was barely enough room between the tip of each paddle and the metal blower edge to squeeze a wrench in to grip the locknut.

Seven of the eight came off okay, and I managed to save nine of 10 knuckles—red ooze revealing the wounded one.

The last nut would not come off regardless of how much I cranked. It was obviously stripped, and the only solution I could see was to find a new torx screw of the same size—with a thick middle flange that hugged the hole in the rubber blade—and then put the hacksaw to work on the stripped one.

I drove east to Ace Hardware and found Bob, a longtime employee.

"It's from the paddle on a snowblower about 25 years old," I said as he examined one of the torx screws I'd managed to remove.

"Can't help you," he said.

"Know any Toro dealers in town?"

"Try Porter's on Center Avenue."

"What about Four Seasons?"

"They might have it. Or Farm & Fleet."

I drove across town to Four Seasons, a west-side place that had worked on my mower. The owner searched a big drawer filled with small baggies of small parts. "Huh. Musta sold the last one. Try Porter's."

"What about Farm & Fleet?"

"They won't have it. I could order one if Porter's doesn't have it."

"Or I could order it online myself."

"True."

"These damned things don't come off easily," I said.

"No, they don't. They're a real bear to tackle."

"The engineer who designed this setup should be shot." I turned to leave but stopped. "My wife wondered why I was working on this today. Told her because I have time and don't want to wait until a snowstorm is rolling in."

"Good idea."

I drove to Porter's Lawn and Power Equipment, on the south side.

At the service counter, an older guy was engaged with a big computer screen. I waited. When he noticed me, he apologized. After he studied the screw, he seemed stumped.

"It holds the paddle on a Toro snowblower about 25 years old," I said.

"Ya got the model number?"

"I didn't think to bring it along," I said, feeling stupid.

He turned to another clerk, a woman, who pointed him in the right direction. From behind a wall of parts, he lugged out a big plastic box with compartments that looked like an average fishing tackle box.

His fishing expedition failed to hook my torx screw. He mumbled and went behind the wall to retrieve another box.

"This one should have it," he said optimistically, but my optimism was fading.

Then he found it. "I need a locknut to go with it," I said, and he found that, too.

"These blades are darn hard to change, with the housing so close to the blade," I told the woman as she rang up my $1.54 purchase. "The engineer who designed this setup should be shot."

"They are frustrating, but our service guys have the job down pretty good," she said.

"Well, I might be back with the whole blower before I'm done," I told her. "My wife wondered why I'm doing this now. Told her 'cause I've got time and there's no snowstorm blowing in."

The woman smiled knowingly as I turned for the door.

Back home, I had Cheryl hold the machine, which gyrated wildly, as I worked the hacksaw, cutting not just through the screw but the nut holding it. Back and forth, back and forth. I paused for a breather and a few choice words as sweat rolled down my chest. I searched my toolboxes but failed to find a new, sharper hacksaw blade. I returned to my labor, pushing and pulling hundreds of times.

When it looked as though I had cut nearly through the screw, I stuck a screwdriver into the groove and hit it with a hammer. It didn't budge, so I sawed some more. Finally, a second whack on the screwdriver with that hammer knocked the nut off and the torx screw head came out.

Now it was time to put the eight torx screws into the extremely tight holes in the new rubber paddles. Hitting them with a hammer didn't pop them in. Finally, I drilled a large hole in a piece of 2-by-4, nosed the end of each torx screw through the paddle hole and into the hole in the 2-by-4, and used a torx bit—a tad smaller than perfect—in my cordless drill driver to spin the screws into place.

Then it was a matter of putting the paddles in position and reattaching the locknuts. Easier said than done. Curse words again filled the air as Cheryl held the machine and I wrestled each screw of each paddle into a hole. The biggest issue was trying to somehow hold the nut in place while I spun the torx screw to get the nut started. My fingers wouldn't fit between the edge of the blade and the metal edge of the housing. Even putting a pliers to the sheet metal and bending it out a tad didn't provide enough room.

At times I felt like I was wrangling an alligator. I managed to get one screw on, but it seemed askew, and I figured I probably stripped that one, too. But the screw head was so tight in the rubber hole that I was able to tighten the nut.

Still, one wouldn't go on, and it was obvious that I needed something besides my torx tool set to win this battle.

"I need to go back to Ace," I told Cheryl. "I need the right size torx bit to fit these screws, or I'll just strip them, and I can't get enough leverage with my torx set."

I took my torx set along because the tools weren't identified by numbers. "I need a torx bit exactly this size," I told Bob while holding up the correct tool.

He found a two-bit set, confident one would be correct. A clerk rang up $4.21, and I was on my way.

The center blade assembly made it difficult to use my bit driver because the handle was too long. I put the bit in my drill driver, and that worked better, but I spun one so fast I stripped the head. But again, the screw was so tight in the rubber paddle that I managed to secure the locknut.

Finally, I had the two toughest to reach, with the narrowest gap between the blade and metal side. Even Cheryl's fingers weren't slender enough to slip between blade and metal to hold the nut in place. "I need Lexi's skinny little fingers," I said of our granddaughter, who lives in Illinois.

Then I hit on a solution. Place the nut in a vice-grip pliers, and lock that pliers into place—nut hovering behind hole—by pinching it with another vice-gripper to the blower's sheet metal side. I was glad I had two vice-grippers rather than having to make a third run to Ace to buy one.

When that last nut went into place, I held up a greasy paw for a high five from Cheryl. It was almost suppertime.

"Maybe you should start it to make sure it's gonna run," she said as we lugged the machine back up the stairs and into the garage.

"Naw," I said confidently. "Replacing the blades has nothing to do with the motor. It'll run fine."

However, you can bet I'll fire up the snowblower, just to be sure, long before that first flake falls.

17
How Wet?

You want to walk in this rain?
You're a real pain.
How wet do you want to get?

This could be quite a slog,
My dear little dog,
How wet do you want to get?

Whatever the weather,
You want to pee on that tree,
How wet do you want to get?

Will you hurry, pick a spot,
And just do your squat?
How wet do you want to get?

Get out of the mud,
You'll track in that crud!
How wet do you want to get?

I have an umbrella,
Get under it, fella,
How wet do you want to get?

SNAKES, SQUIRRELS & BEARS, OH MY!

I'm feeling all soggy,
You persistent doggy,
How wet do you want to get?

Even my glasses are wet;
Will you hurry, dear pet?
How wet do you want to get?

That rumble was thunder,
You cause me to wonder,
Just how wet do you want to get?

Trapper, just pee,
Make this your last tree.
How wet do you want us to get?

18
Boat Be Gone

A lifelong fisherman, I always dreamed of having my own boat. When I bought a beautiful open lot on the Wisconsin River north of Muscoda, two hours from home, that desire tipped toward need. How could a guy take advantage of the fishing opportunities right in front of his property without a boat to get away from the sandy shallows?

My smile was as wide as the 14-foot Alumacraft when I first towed the vintage 1979 boat home to Janesville.

I got it from my uncle Fran Klecker, with help from Mom.

The troubles I towed home with the boat, however, were evident from my first tug on the Mariner recoil starter's pull rope.

Fran thought the 15-horse motor wasn't pulling the cooling water through correctly, so I took it to a dealer in nearby Newville. He checked it over and declared it fine. I've never been mechanically inclined, but my classmate Mike Taylor is. Just to be sure the motor was okay, I towed the boat to Mike's Jefferson home, where he and I dismantled and double-checked its functions.

The motor wasn't the only issue. I blew a fuse before leaving the dealership and couldn't keep the trailer's taillights working. My brother Tom, our family's Mr. Fix-It, replaced the trailer wiring.

Still, the fuse blew again when I backed up. That led Tom to believe I needed a new electrical trailer harness for the truck. Replacing that solved the problem.

I bought an oversized canvas cover at the local Farm & Fleet and parked the boat on my river property. But when I made my next trip up there a few weeks later, rain had formed a pool of heavy water, which rotted and ripped the cover. The back of the boat had filled with scummy, stinky water. I paid $7 to ship the cover—under a five-year warranty—to the Seattle manufacturer. The company sent me a new one, which I wound up returning to the store for a refund.

Instead, I bought a large plastic tarp for those times I planned to leave the boat at the river. I installed a post with a winch a few yards up from the usual water line to pull the boat ashore. Leaving it there, I figured, would prove simpler and faster than trailering it each time I wanted to drive over to fish.

Despite frequent boat maintenance problems, Cheryl and I did enjoy a few fun times on the Wisconsin River. Here, we took our dog Trapper for a ride.

A couple of weeks of heavy rains fell, and my phone rang. It was Brian, the next-door neighbor and attorney who had used a tape measure to help me determine the lot lines and then did the closing when I bought the place.

"Greg, it seems the water rose high enough to float your boat; now it's tipped against a tree."

"Gee," I said, "thanks for letting me know. I left a can of gas in it. Can you retrieve it so it doesn't leak?"

"Sure thing."

Brian was fast becoming one of my best friends, and this was only Year One of boat ownership.

Frustrations in Year Two started not with the boat but with the trailer connections. While towing Mike's boat to Canada, we had to catch Farm & Fleet in Madison before it closed at 9 p.m. to again replace the truck's trailer harness.

That year, my dad and uncle installed an Anchormate on the boat's bow so I could crank up the anchor while seated near the rear-tiller motor when I was out on the river alone. Unfortunately, they had to mount a pulley slightly to the side of the light mounted on the point of the bow. With the strong river currents, the anchor rope kept slipping off of the pulley and catching, and I still had to climb past my tackle box, bait bucket, net, cooler, and rods and reels to free it while the motor idled and the boat drifted swiftly downstream.

In addition, mice found the boat, with its plastic tarp, a cozy hideout. They chewed into the Styrofoam floats under the seats, emerging to greet me as I fished.

By Year Three, I had built a skid of treated lumber and carpet pieces for sliding the boat even farther ashore. But heavy June rains again fell.

"The water's too high to fish, so don't bother driving over," Brian advised me.

When Cheryl and I went on vacation, more rain again sagged the tarp, pooling water and flooding the back of the boat. Fearing it might sink, Brian cut the chain lock and dragged it onto the trailer, which I had left locked, leaving him unable to hook it to his truck.

I had chained the skid, too, but it broke apart in the floodwaters and floated toward Prairie du Chien.

From a catalog, I bought a gadget to prop up the tarp, but the weight of rainwater bent the cheap plastic device, rendering it useless. I salvaged the accompanying straps and attached them to a prop I built out of wood. But in October when I went to retrieve the boat for winter storage, I had to bust out a large pool of frozen water. By then the motor was leaking, too, so I took it to the dealer, who replaced a cracked seal in the lower unit.

I was getting the hint: I was spending more time and energy getting my prized boat prepped and launched each spring and stored away each autumn than I was using it.

Each winter I stored the boat in my parents' extra garage in Minocqua. When I went to retrieve it in spring of Year Four, Dad and I decided to modify the position of the Anchormate. First, we found one roller so worn from the improper angle of the rope winding through it that we had to buy replacement parts. Then we used plastic tie wraps to realign the pulley atop the light. It seemed cobbled together but worked fine.

While doing that, however, I checked the lights and found the battery dead. Worse, it wouldn't hold a charge. A dealer charged $53 for a new one.

I towed the boat home and put it in my garage, awaiting that first trip to the river. Meanwhile, my new truck sat in the driveway, and each thunderstorm brought fears of hail damage to the vehicle.

A small puddle on the garage floor suggested the motor was leaking again. I'd also stripped the screw on the oil drain in the lower unit. Two weeks at a dealership cost more than $200 for a seal kit.

It was becoming obvious that the boat's drain on my wallet didn't match its value. Besides, Brian had long since replaced his flat-bottom boat with a newer, faster model. Whenever he and I went fishing, my boat sat on the lot, under the tarp.

In Year Five, I left the boat at my parents' place. When fishing season opened, Dad and I rolled it to the street and stuck a "for sale" sign on it. The first interested guy paid my asking price—$100 less than my purchase price despite the addition of the Anchormate.

It has often been said that the two happiest days of a fisherman's life are the day he buys a boat and the day he sells it.

I can't argue with that.

19
Customer "Service" Is a Contradiction in Terms

After I retired from newspaper editing at age 59, people asked, "Have you been golfing? Fishing?" Those first two years, I did little of either. Instead, calling and emailing to arrange finances, medical care, and home improvements filled most days. I learned that in today's world of commerce, "customer service" is a contradiction in terms.

Please, someone tell me: Do I have a "Do Not Service" label tattooed to my forehead?

Let me count the transgressions.

One: After several years of recommending Humana, our insurance consultant told us my wife's plan covered her three prescriptions free. Humana would mail them.

While irked that he didn't tell us this before, I did a little dance around the kitchen. No more standing in line to pay at a pharmacy while the sick slob behind me sneezes and coughs without covering his mouth!

I asked my wife's doctors to switch her prescriptions to Humana. She was running low on one drug, and Humana's processing time made it a squeeze. She went without it for a week, and I called Humana again.

"We never heard back from her doctor," a Humana employee told me.

I had to call the clinic and get a short-term prescription at the pharmacy until Humana's shipment arrived.

Two: At a home show, I stopped at a booth with a sign that promised, "Long-Lasting Ceramic Coating" for exterior wood.

"Our house is brick, but I'd like an estimate on the soffits and roof trim," I told a representative.

"We can have someone there at 9:30 Friday."

"Sounds good," I said.

The guy didn't show up. I called at 10 and 10:30 and again at 12:30.

Finally, at 4:30, the estimator called back. "Sorry about the miscommunication," he said, "and now it's too dark to come out. Can you describe your project?"

After I explained it, he said, "Our minimum fee is $5,000."

"What? Nobody suggested that! My project isn't worth that much."

Later, I wrote a complaint to the owner but never heard back.

Three: Cheryl already owned our home when we wed, and our banker noticed only her name remained on the deed. We anticipated a simple trip to the Rock County Register of Deeds Office to fill out paperwork.

"We can't give you the forms," a clerk told us. "You must download them from our website, and similar forms from the state's website. You might want a lawyer's help."

We thought it a good idea when we learned the deed still listed my wife's former name, as well as a mortgage we'd paid off. Our lawyer drew up the paperwork. We paid him $125.

Four: For decades, Cheryl and I visited different dentists. I learned that hers offered a discount for cash.

I later learned—only by asking—that mine did, too.

Five: I called my auto dealership's body shop. "I need you to fix a squeak I keep hearing inside the hatch of my Honda CR-V."

"Our manager is out all week," a clerk said. "Could you bring it in at 7:30 a.m. next Tuesday?"

"Sure."

I had Cheryl tail me so she could drive me home rather than waiting. We got there, and the shop had no record of the appointment and no time to work on it that day.

Six: I booked three hotel rooms halfway to Ontario for five fishing buddies and I to stop at on our trip.

Days before leaving, I called to ask, "Any chance we could leave a car in your lot all week?"

"Sure," the clerk said, only mentioning in passing that we were somehow booked for six rooms, not three.

Seven: I booked a local hotel because I thought relatives would use it for our anniversary. But they later decided to drive home after the celebration.

"I need to cancel my reservation," I told a desk clerk days ahead of the gathering.

"That's fine."

My credit card got billed anyway. I had to call back to get the charge refunded.

Eight: Cheryl and I wanted to reach the stadium turnstiles early for a Milwaukee Brewers game to ensure we'd get the right sizes in a Sunday jersey giveaway. Instead of grilling during a tailgate party, we decided to take sub sandwiches.

I called Saturday to ask what time the sub shop opened Sunday.

"At 7 a.m.," a perky-sounding female told me.

"Wow, that's pretty early, but great," I said.

When we arrived the next day, we learned it usually opens at 7 a.m. but not until *9 a.m.* on Sundays.

Nine: We were having a new fireplace damper installed because the old, rusty one didn't close properly and let in virtual clouds of stink bugs. I had to contact the contractor repeatedly to first get an estimate, then get him to measure for parts.

Ten: At midyear, we reduced an investment draw so our income stayed low enough to receive an Affordable Care Act tax credit. We filled out paperwork at our bank. But our statement the next month showed not a reduced deposit but none at all.

"I don't understand how this happened," our investment adviser said. "We received notice from the investment company that the paperwork was approved, but for some reason I don't understand, it was later rejected without notice.

"This has never happened before," she assured us.

We returned to the bank and filled out fresh paperwork.

Eleven: Cheryl's doctor suggested the new two-dose Shingrix vaccine. Cheryl hates needles, so I made the first appointment. We were told to call for the second one between two and six months later. I called two months later.

"We don't have the second dose in. Call back next week."

I did so and was told the same thing and advised of an expected, long-term nationwide shortage.

"Why did you give her the first dose when you were expecting a shortage?" I asked a nurse.

She had no good answer.

I waited two weeks before calling again. This time, a different nurse said they had three doses, and she'd check to see if they'd been spoken for. She put me on hold.

"You're in luck," she said when she returned. "I'll put your wife's name on one of them."

Twelve: We had a Wales, Wisconsin, company install a new air conditioner and got a postcard four months later from an unfamiliar Milwaukee electric company—addressed to "Gary" Peck—saying we must call City Hall to schedule an inspection. I called the air-conditioning company and learned that, yes, this Milwaukee company subcontracted the electrical work.

I called the city inspection department, and a clerk asked me the name of the person who did the work. "I don't know, I have only a postcard saying I must call you for an inspection."

"Do you have a phone number?"

"It's not on the postcard."

"I'll relay this to the building inspector."

Two days later, the building inspector called to make an appointment. "This subcontractor used indoor wiring outdoors and must redo it," he said.

Weeks passed before the correct material was installed.

Thirteen: I called the plumber who installed our toilet and asked about a simple fix for water fluctuations.

"That should work," he said of my idea, but after I tried it, it did the opposite. The toilet got too little water, and I twice left messages requesting a service visit.

Finally, I figured out how to fix it myself and left him a "disregard" message.

Fourteen: I called a garden center that has been treating our tree for emerald ash borers every two years. I didn't realize three years had slipped past since the last treatment.

"I tried calling a year ago and got no response," the applicator said. "Did you change phone numbers?"

"We've had the same phone number for decades," I said.

Fifteen: We wanted to switch my wife's credit union savings to a certificate of deposit. I called on a Friday about the rates and was asked if I wanted to stop in or make an appointment.

"We have errands, so we'll just stop in."

No receptionist was there, and we stood in a long line. A teller took our phone number. "Someone will call you," she said before we drove home.

No one did, and in frustration I emailed our bank to ask about rates. It appeared that the credit union's were better, so I replied that we'd keep this pot of money there despite my irritation. This time, I made a Tuesday appointment. The investment adviser apologized because the receptionist was out on medical leave, the main office didn't send a substitute, and they were swamped Friday with Social Security payments, etc.

"I never got your message," she said. "I'm sorry about that, too."

We opened a CD at 1.8 percent. We returned home to an email from our bank suggesting the credit union's "2.0 rate" was indeed better than the bank's. I called the credit union's investment adviser to ask why we didn't get that rate.

"That's a different type of investment."

"What's the difference?"

"The other investment allows withdrawals without penalty and additions."
I said, "So, it's better two ways?"
"Yes."
"So why didn't you suggest that?"
"Because you said you wanted a CD."

Sixteen: Not the biggest issue but perhaps most annoying, I asked my newspaper, my former employer, for a short vacation stop over the Fourth of July holiday because we went north to visit Mom.
"Please deliver Monday's and Tuesday's papers Thursday."
I didn't get them Thursday and had to call that day *and* Friday before getting the missing papers.

My ongoing to-do list beckons on the kitchen counter. It snares me daily, leaving little time to gauge customer service at the golf course. Maybe more companies should consider hiring part-time workers from a generation that understood the value of treating customers well.

In the meantime, I'm going to gaze in the bathroom mirror and check my forehead.

20
I "Bearly" Slept a Wink!

"Jim," I said while nudging my snoring friend and coworker. "I think something's gnawing on our packs under the canoe."

"I think you're right," he mumbled.

Jim Leute and I had pitched camp on a rocky bluff. It was our final night during my only trip into the Boundary Waters Canoe Area. We ate supper, fished, then fell asleep with our food pack dangling securely—at least we hoped—from a rope tied to a tree branch.

A light sleeper, I had slept fitfully each night of the four-day trip. Comfort was impossible on my thin air mattress and small pillow. This final night, I awoke to the sounds of chewing. Was it a bear? A raccoon? Some other creature?

I lay there thinking back to that night in Ontario, when fishing buddy Mike Taylor—who slept in his van because "You snore too much"—left me alone in a tent, and we'd placed a can of spent cooking grease in our campsite trash barrel, and I awoke to heavy footfalls and heavy breathing and stayed frozen in my sleeping bag as a bear tipped that barrel and enjoyed a midnight snack.

On this night, as Jim and I lay side by side, a gentle breeze and moonlight shining through tree limbs created eerie shadows that danced atop the tent. Were those waves lapping at the shoreline or was an animal lapping up our foodstuff?

I grabbed a small flashlight and—despite fears that I might wind up face to face with a bear—stumbled barefoot into the damp darkness.

SNAKES, SQUIRRELS & BEARS, OH MY!

Jim Leute poses for a photo while cooking our supper in the Boundary Waters Canoe Area. We hung food packs in a tree to try to keep bears from getting to them.

I shined the light on the canoe and yelled, "Hey."

My shout startled our intruder, which seemingly had fallen from the tree and plopped onto the overturned canoe. The animal—quite small if a bear—ambled toward the water ten yards away.

"What was it?" Jim asked.

"I don't know," I replied. "A raccoon, a beaver, a bear cub? I couldn't tell."

I slipped back into the tent, quickly zipping the opening behind me to keep marauding mosquitoes from invading.

"What time is it?" I asked.

"Three o'clock."

We lay quietly, but it took only a minute for our visitor to return. We heard it thump the canoe.

"Hey!" Jim and I yelled in unison.

It scampered off, only to return soon after.

Flashlight in hand, I again slipped outside.

This time, I saw a leaf-filled tree branch, perhaps eight feet long, heading toward the water.

"It's a damn beaver," I said.

73

Jim Leute drinks in a spectacular sunrise over a lake we camped on in the Boundary Waters Canoe Area.

"They never quit, those guys."

We fell asleep to his gnawing. When we emerged at daybreak, the only evidence was two sticks, stripped of their bark, lying near shore.

Stowing our undisturbed food pack and other gear in the intact canoe, we paddled toward our truck, recapping our nighttime encounter with a harmless intruder and chuckling at the memory of that damn beaver.

21
One Sneaky Snake

"Hey, Cornwallis escaped from his cage," stepson Adam announced.
I jumped from my chair. "What? How did that happen?"

"He must have bumped the lid with his nose until it slid open just enough for him to slip out."

"Well, find him!"

Adam grew up with allergies and asthma, but these didn't deter his passion for pets. His mother, Cheryl, had a cairn terrier before I came into their lives, and she and I had a second one together when Adam still lived with us. The teenaged Adam also had a hedgehog named Oakley. Though prickly, it was sort of cute and didn't bother me.

Cornwallis was a harmless corn snake, but I've never been fond of snakes, even one caged in an aquarium with a sliding screened ceiling. My fears weren't assuaged by watching Cornwallis eat. He ate mice—live ones. Once a month, Adam placed one in the snake's cage. The three-foot snake slowly snuck toward the cowering rodent until it pounced, snaring its snout in his jaws and quickly wrapping his length around the hapless mouse, whose shaking legs splayed in all directions. Slowly, Cornwallis swallowed the mouse whole, the snake's body resembling an old, badly bulging inner tube.

Adam and Cheryl searched the house for this escape artist, turned up nothing, and gave up. I wasn't pleased.

"It's no big deal," Cheryl said. "He'll eventually turn up."

"No way," I said. It wasn't that I feared Cornwallis might mistake my big toe for his next meal. Instead, I told her, "I'm not going to be relaxing, watching TV, and have that thing slither across my leg and give me a heart attack."

I couldn't rest knowing that snake was somewhere in the house. So when my own son, Josh, eight years younger than Adam, came to visit that night, we picked up the search.

We started in the basement because that's where Adam kept Cornwallis's cage. Our home, built in the 1940s, has never been the focus of the Netflix show "Get Organized." Cluttered chaos defines our cellar. Suffice it to say, this disarray leaves plenty of spots for a sneaky snake to hide.

Josh and I searched high and low. Using flashlights, we scanned shelves, looking above, below, and behind an assortment of possessions that Cheryl and I never use, seldom use, or might use again.

I pulled rolls of wrapping paper and bins and boxes of Christmas wrapping supplies off a shelf. When I opened a box of used but still useable ribbons, there sat Cornwallis, curled up, his brown tones contrasting with the brightly colored bows, enjoying his dark, warm hideout.

Adam returned him to his cage and slid the lid back into place.

But several days later, this reptilian Houdini went AWOL again. And again, Adam and his mom gave up the search without success, and Josh and I picked up where they left off.

Cornwallis, however, wasn't in that box of bows this time. He wasn't in a lot of other places in which we'd looked previously either. Minutes turned into more than an hour. Josh and I were running out of places to search.

I was scratching my head in my workshop when Josh said, "What about in there?" He was pointing to a vinyl accordion-like PVC duct hose that Adam's father once used to suck up sawdust. I never used the hose, vented outside, so I'd plugged the end of it with an old towel to keep cold outside air from coming inside.

"I doubt it," I said.

"Maybe he slipped past that towel and is sitting in there because it's warm now," Josh reasoned.

"Could be," I said, scooping the end of the four-inch hose off the concrete floor and pulling at the towel.

SNAKES, SQUIRRELS & BEARS, OH MY!

And there lay Cornwallis, curled up, minding his own business, nice and cozy in a warm, dark place.

Again Adam returned him to his cage. But I wasn't about to be snookered a third time by this slippery snake. I went back to my workshop and retrieved a small C-clamp to pinch the edge of the lid to the side of the cage. That put a halt to this Houdini's magic disappearing act.

22
Friend's Foibles Put the Fun in Fishing

My friend Dave Janisch had yet to show up. We had agreed to meet at 9 a.m. at the public boat launch on Delavan Lake, but 9:15, then 9:30 came, and I quit pacing the pier and sat in my car. It was the era before cell phones, and I thought about leaving, but I was certain Dave was coming.

Finally, just before 10, he showed up, boat in tow.

"What took you so long?"

"I no more than got down the street," he said, "and got a flat tire on the trailer."

Sure, I thought. It was probably flat for weeks and, Dave being Dave, he never bothered to check it before heading out the driveway.

As we fished, I recalled other incidents. Like the time Dave, Mike Taylor, and I—three high school buddies—went to Canada and Dave, as usual, was using an old rod and reel likely inherited from his father.

We were casting for northern pike in a sun-splashed bay, and Dave got a hit. He set the hook and fought a modest-size fish. It stayed deep, and suddenly Dave's reel slipped off the rod, bounced off the edge of the aluminum boat, and fell into the clear water, plunging as deep as the pike.

Mike and I laughed so hard we fell out of our seats as Dave retrieved the reel, grabbing line a couple of feet at a time, the fish still fighting at the other end of the tangled mess. Sure enough, Dave managed to land both the reel and the pike. Mike and I weren't surprised.

SNAKES, SQUIRRELS & BEARS, OH MY!

Dave Janisch nodded off with a beer in hand moments before he landed the biggest walleye during our first trip to Ontario, Canada. In the background is Mike Taylor. We became friends while attending Marshall High School.

I recalled, too, the day Mike and I started calling Dave "Dad." That nickname arose on our first trip to Canada together. Dave is a couple of years older than Mike and me, and he often acted many years older.

A photo in my fishing album shows the incident. Dave, shirtless, budding belly rolls obvious, leaned back against a boat cushion. He sported sunglasses, sideburns, and a mustache, and he'd nodded off in the sunshine, clutching a beer bottle in one hand. His rod tip lay propped between his toes.

I used my rod tip to tap the end of Dave's rod so he'd think he had a bite.

"Knock it off," he said groggily, pushing his sunglasses back in place with one finger and again nodding off.

Just after I snapped that photo, a big walleye hit. Dave awoke in time to land that one, too, the largest of the trip.

In more recent years, I fished with Dave at his place on the Menominee River near Pembine, on the Wisconsin side of the Upper Peninsula. We usually drove up separately, but this time we rode together in the vehicle his wife normally used.

Dave opened his garage door before we left. "Gotta add some oil to this rig," he said. He stumbled toward a shelf in a two-car garage so stuffed that no vehicle fit. He complained about how his wife's missionary material filled the garage. Take that out, and you still wouldn't get a car in, I reasoned silently.

After pouring in a quart of oil, Dave said, "We'd better stop and get some more in town."

"How low is it?"

"I'm not sure."

The engine took two more quarts, and I shook my head wondering how he could let his wife drive to work in such a jalopy.

Halfway to Pembine, Dave said, "I'd better slow down."

"How fast you going?" I said, leaning over to gaze at the speedometer.

"That doesn't work," he said. "Gotta use my cell phone to monitor speed."

I sat in silence.

A little later, Dave said, "We should stop for gas."

"How low's she getting?"

"Don't know," he said. "The gas gauge doesn't work."

I shook my head again. Somehow, we made it to Pembine and back without needing a tow truck.

While there, however, we quit fishing early one day for a run into town for more minnows. Loading the boat, Dave hurriedly jumped into the vehicle.

"What about the trailer lights?"

"Don't bother with them," he said. "Let's hurry before the bait shop closes."

We made it to the store in time, but as Dave veered off the highway, a trucker behind us laid on his horn.

"Screw you," Dave spewed in reply. "I signaled."

"Dave, you don't even have the trailer lights hooked up."

"Oh ya, I forgot."

Dave is nothing if not a good, old-fashioned, self-deprecating storyteller.

So, he was more than willing to share the foibles he experienced one weekend with another buddy at his place up north.

First, his friend lost his wallet while they hiked through the woods. Then, Dave's motor quit as they were boating upstream from the dam. Dave being Dave, he didn't have a paddle aboard, as regulations require.

Dave and his buddy managed to dog paddle to shore by hand before the boat drifted over the dam. Then, Dave had to drag the boat back upriver, against a strong current, as he stumbled along the shoreline for just a mile or two.

On the trip's last evening, a storm blew in. Dave, his friend, and their families played cards as lightning flashed, thunder roared, and wind and heavy rain rattled the trailer.

Suddenly, an enormous crash startled them. The next morning, they stepped outside, only to discover that a large pine had fallen. Fortunately, it missed the vehicles, as well as the tents they'd pitched for the kids. But it had fallen across the driveway.

Dave and his buddy spent the entire day hacking away with the only logical tool Dave had available, a hatchet.

That's Dave, my "always-prepared" buddy, who, truth be told, spent his entire career in law enforcement and worked for years as an undercover detective.

23
In the Kitchen, It's Too Hot or Too Cold

Bruce Kufahl was a high school buddy who stood up at my first wedding, and he and his new bride, Sue, threw a bachelor party for me in 1980 at their ranch home in Lake Mills.

Photos from that autumn evening show the hosts and more of my high school friends, many in various states of overindulgence. Two pictures also show a party cake with a rather revealing figurine atop it. Sue dubbed it the "boob cake."

The cleavage didn't cause any scandal, however. Rather, bringing unwanted attention is what happened to the remains of that cake.

"Oh, I remember that incident well!" Sue recalled, nearly 40 years later. "After everyone left the party, I was trying to quickly clean up everything. Being that Bruce and I were only married a month, I didn't have any container to put the boob cake in. Without thinking, I stuck it in the oven."

A few days later, Sue planned to bake Bruce a birthday cake.

"I preheated the oven and was busy getting things put together for the cake. My back was to the oven. I turned around and saw lots of smoke pouring out of the oven."

The oven had no window and was quite old.

"I still didn't remember the boob cake. I freaked out and called the fire department, thinking my oven was on fire. Just then, Bruce got home and as he was getting out of his car I yelled 'The oven's on fire. The fire trucks are on their way.'

"He had a puzzled look on his face! One fireman was in the area when the call came through, so he drove to the house in his private vehicle. He went to the oven, felt around the door and opened it. That's when I saw the boob cake, which was on a piece of cardboard burning up, little flames coming off it."

The fireman removed the rack with the cake and dumped the charred mess on the backyard grass.

"It was too late to call off the fire trucks because I could hear the sirens coming," Sue said.

When the trucks arrived, the firefighter who dumped the cake explained how he already solved the problem.

"They all got a good laugh, but they were also very kind. I just kept saying 'I've only been married a month.' They heard about the birthday cake that I was going to bake, so one of the firemen yelled out to the guys still at the trucks that 'She burned the birthday cake.'"

The firefighters used a fan to blow the smoke out of the kitchen, but not before opening the old window over the sink, only to have the window slam down again and break.

"I was embarrassed, but it has made for a good story many times over the years," Sue told me. "My brother, who at the time was a full-time fireman for the city of Waukesha, really got a good laugh out of it."

I could imagine the headline in that week's Lake Mills newspaper: "Newlywed burns birthday cake."

Almost every family has a kitchen disaster, one that lives in infamy and is recalled to rollicking laughter as the years tick by. Cheryl and I cooked up our own kitchen debacle 16 years later, a few months before marrying in Hawaii. Here's the recipe we used:

—Invite 27 family members over for a 1 p.m. Christmas dinner.

—Buy two turkeys because one large one won't be enough.

—Stuff both birds, place them in separate slow cookers at midnight and hit the sack.

—Awaken at 6 a.m. and check Small Bird, which we feared might burn, but don't head to the basement to check on Big Bird, which we assumed was doing fine. Besides, the pleasing aroma of roast turkey was wafting through the house.

—Check on both birds at 8:30 a.m. and discover—to our horror—that we forgot to plug in the cooker for Big Bird.

—Head to four grocery stores in search of a ham or something that will cook quickly. Learn that none is open.

—Call all the relatives, enduring laughter as we ask if they can come for supper instead.

Most of Cheryl's family admitted later that supper proved less hectic and allowed them to visit other relatives earlier in the day.

But you can be sure that Cheryl's three sisters—notorious for holiday goofs that come back to haunt them—never forgot this flub. Every time it comes up, Cheryl and I feel like, well, turkeys.

24
Molly's Frightening First Night

"There's an ad here in the State Journal for a female cairn puppy at a breeder's place in Portage," I told Cheryl. "We could make a triangular trip, going first to Muscoda and from there to Portage to see it."
"Sounds great," she said. "But you know if we do, we're bringing it home."
"I understand."
That Saturday, we planned to drive two hours to mow the lawn on our Wisconsin River property near Muscoda. Two months earlier, we'd put down our previous cairn terrier, Trapper, because he was full of cancer. That loss left us heartbroken.
After mowing, we traveled a winding path along the river valley's bluffs northeast to Portage and the breeder's rural home.
"I named her Molly," she told us. "I don't usually sell a pup after I name it, but she's nearly four months old."
We joined the woman, her husband, and a pack of young and mature dogs scurrying around their deck and backyard. Almost all were cairns. Among them were Molly's brother, a spitfire half her size who was already sold. The breeder had nursed the little fellow with a bottle although she doubted he would survive. He was friendly despite a loud bark, which suggested a large attitude that belied his small stature.
In contrast, Molly seemed sweet but timid, shy and reluctant even to let us pick her up.
Sitting in a big deck chair, the man tossed a stuffed animal into the yard for the dogs to chase. I marveled at the speed of Molly, who leaped off the deck and romped after the toy.

"Aren't you afraid they'll run out in the road?" I asked the woman. "The older dogs know to stay away from the road, and the pups stay with them."

Molly was a cute little black ball of fur when she came home that first night from Portage. But that innocent look could be deceiving.

We didn't have one in mind but liked the name Molly. Because she seemed to perk up every time someone called her by name, we thought it best to keep it. We paid the woman and happily drove off with Molly, wearing big smiles on our faces.

Daylight was fading when we got home, where we realized that, at about eight pounds, Molly was too tiny for Trapper's collar. Trapper, after all, was about 20 pounds at his heaviest—big for a cairn.

"She should do her business," Cheryl suggested.

I looked at that black face framing a dark brindle coat, thought back to that fast pup I watched chase that stuffed toy, and reluctantly agreed. We sat Molly in our side yard, between the driveway and a hedge at our lot line, and stood on either side of her as she sniffed the grass.

We hoped she would at least pee. She didn't feel the urge, however.

We took her inside to play and get acquainted with her new home. We were exhausted and ready for bed as darkness was setting in, but Cheryl thought it best to give Molly one more chance out in the yard.

"Okay," I again said with hesitation. I should have followed my instincts telling me this was a bad idea.

We sat Molly down, without so much as a collar to identify her, and she again sniffed around. A large dog several doors down the street started barking.

SNAKES, SQUIRRELS & BEARS, OH MY!

Molly, ready for a walk in her winter coat, has become an elderly dog with much gray around her face. It's hard to believe our time with her has passed so quickly—she turned 12 as this book went into production.

Molly looked startled and scooted on her short but quick legs toward the sidewalk parallel to the street. Fortunately, I had sneakers on rather than sandals, and I ran after her into the street and around the neighbor's massive terrace maple, trying to head her off as she scurried down the sidewalk.

However, she bolted across the street to a neighbor's corner lot.

I chased after her, but Molly sprinted across the other street to yet another corner lot, toward a row of overgrown hydrangeas.

My mind raced along with my legs: In this dim light, we might never find her if she dives into those flowers, and she doesn't have any identification! "Molly, Molly, come here girl," I called, trying to hide the frantic feeling in my gut.

Molly plunged into the hydrangeas with me in pursuit. I got there, lost sight of her, then caught a glimpse as she rocketed into the adjoining yard. I tore after her. She doubled back. Looping the corner lot, she headed for that home's detached garage.

Molly would much prefer going bicycling with us than going for a walk. With biking, she doesn't have to exercise, and she's pretty lazy.

The homeowners often sat in lawn chairs with the overhead door open and a light on at night. There they were, and the sudden sight of strangers startled Molly. She skidded to a cautious halt.

Cheryl and I managed to close in on her. Molly tried zipping behind me. I made a grab for her, catching one hind leg. I gathered her in and held on tight.

"I don't know whose heart is beating faster—hers or mine," I gasped as Cheryl and I headed home. "I'm going to the grocery to find a collar that'll fit her."

Not that we needed it, for things changed as Molly soon settled into her new surroundings, matured, and mellowed.

Molly has proven to be the sweetest dog I've ever been around. But in contrast to Trapper, Molly is lazy. Trapper, always eager for a walk, would drag his leash down the hall from the closet to the door. But when we call Molly, we find her lying in the living room, looking as if to say, "What? You need to go for another walk already?"

Molly does love to go bicycling with us though. She rides in a little basket on the back of my bike or our tandem as Cheryl and I get all the exercise. Of course, knowing we sometimes stop for ice cream does add to Molly's enthusiasm.

If Cheryl and I plan to work in the yard, Molly prefers to sit inside. She remains cautious. She's skittish around other dogs. I sometimes call her "Nervous Nelly." She answers to many other nicknames, too, including Molly Mae, Moll Flanders, Scooby, George, Goober, Gertrude, Goofy, Babe, BooBoo, Baba Looey, Killer, and even—after she has shred another tissue or napkin, clean or used—Shithead.

Just like Trapper, Molly jumps against the metal screen door saver to bark at a passing dog or human. And while she might chase a squirrel or another dog, we no longer fear she will run away.

Once, while mowing the front yard, I heard barking. I stopped the mower and noticed the front screen door hanging wide open. Obviously, it hadn't been latched. Molly had jumped against the door and it popped open. Rather than making a second bid at a great escape, she stood in the living room woofing at it, as if to say, "Dad, this isn't right."

Yes, Molly has come a long way from that first frightening night.

25
Rummaging into the Human Psyche

The air hung heavy with a damp smell on that mid-June morning. Dew clung to the grass when the first car stopped for my rummage sale. Coffee cup in hand, I gazed out the window. Other vehicles soon stopped, as well. It was twenty minutes before my advertised opening. Still, I decided to step out and roll up the garage doors.

As I did, the waiting motorists leaped out of their cars and trucks and raced to look at and pick over the discarded possessions of my life.

I'm married, but these weren't rejects from "our life"; my wife wanted nothing to do with the sale, so I decided to sell only "my" stuff, including unused tools and camping and fishing equipment.

The rush was on. I wanted $50 for the riding John Deere pedal tractor for which I spent more than $100 to give to my dad as a humorous Christmas gift. When my grandson, Remy, was old enough to ride it, Dad returned it to me, and the youngster pedaled it around until he outgrew it. Now, with Dad gone, it was time to part with the green toy.

"Will you take $30 for it?" asked one of the first shoppers, a middle-aged gentleman.

"I don't know. It's in good shape, and I think it's worth more than that. How about $40?"

"I'll give you $35," the guy countered.

"Okay," I said reluctantly, wondering, with eight hours of potential sales time in each of the next two days, whether someone else might offer more.

SNAKES, SQUIRRELS & BEARS, OH MY!

This initial sale was only the first in a flurry of activity as coins and dollar bills flew into and out of my cardboard cash box. I was glad I had the foresight to stock plenty of coins and small bills for making change.

Maybe I priced some items too low, but I wanted everything to sell; my plan was to take nothing back to the house, basement, or garage but to haul it to Goodwill. A quarter here and a dollar there would be better than giving each item away. I planned, if I raked in enough, to buy a Bose stereo for our living room.

While my wife busied herself inside, I dealt with a steady stream of customers all morning on what evolved into a picturesque day. Several fishing rods and reels went, as did unused tackle boxes filled with jigs and lures that I deemed ineffective at enticing fish.

A Coleman camping stove sold, as did a lantern in a plastic carrying case. Someone bought my camp hatchet and an old sleeping bag.

Shoppers snapped up assorted tools like they'd just discovered golden nuggets in some mountain stream. Snatched quickly were screwdrivers, a rivet set I never used, and an old power drill I no longer needed now that I had a cordless drill and driver. Whether to part with a certain tool sometimes posed a difficult decision, and, sure enough, after selling my seldom-used Sawzall, I needed one on a project a few months later.

As the shopping pace waned closer to lunchtime, a car driven by a woman pulled up. A young man stepped out and limped into my garage.

After a few minutes scanning tables of odds and ends, he picked up a computer mouse pad that depicted former Green Bay Packer running back Ahman Green. The price was 50 cents.

"I don't have any money but would like this," the man said. "Could I have it?"

I was almost too stunned to respond. I sucked in a breath and said, "No."

He tossed the pad back on the table and headed for the car as I shook my head. Why, I wondered, would someone visit rummage sales without any money? Did this gimpy young fellow curry sympathy from other sellers?

Then another woman pulled up. I noticed her Illinois license plate. She browsed the tables and dozens of items spread along the driveway. A twelve-foot aluminum extension ladder caught her attention. Since buying LeafGuard gutters, and owning a sixteen-footer, I no longer used the twelve-footer. It just collected dust in my garage, so I priced it at $40.

"I have to call my handyman to see if this is the right length for his use," she said. She whipped out her cell phone. A few minutes later, she hung up and turned to me. "I don't know; he thinks he needs one longer than that."

"Well, I'll sell it to you for $30 if you want it," I said.

She hemmed and hawed, then reviewed my other goodies again. "I guess I'll just take this," she said, holding an old picture frame priced at 75 cents. "Can you break a $100 bill?"

"Gee, I think so," I said, knowing full well I could cash it but wondering whether she might be working some con that would net her $99.25 in cash for a fake $100 bill. I hesitated but decided to make the change after deciding to jot down her license number before she drove off.

I was munching a sandwich as a guy pulled up and started studying the remains of the day. He looked familiar.

"Wow," he said, "you really sold a lot of stuff!"

"Yup."

"I stopped early this morning and liked what I saw, but I was running late for work. I'm on my lunch break now and wanted to see what you still had." He picked up a pair of pliers. "I could tell you really had everything priced to sell."

"I tried to. None of this stuff's going back inside."

An older fellow, he seemed a friendly sort with an engaging smile and personality. He said he sometimes runs rummage sales himself. I told him about the gimpy guy who wanted the mouse pad for free, and about the woman who considered the ladder but then bought a 75-cent item with a $100 bill.

"Rummage sales are really a window to the human psyche," he said.

"You can say that again."

"Everyone wants a bargain. At one of my sales, I had 10 cents on a ceramic coffee cup. A woman asked if I'd sell it for a nickel. I said 'Lemme see that.' She handed it over, I studied it a second, then dropped it on the garage floor. It shattered, of course."

I chuckled.

"The woman stood there stunned, looking at me. I said, 'Lady, if it's not worth a dime, it's not worth a nickel either.'"

I laughed again.

He waved and stepped toward his car. "Have a nice day!"

"Already has been," I said. I could almost hear sweet melodies from that Bose stereo.

26
Please Stop if You See Me Stranded by the Road

I hate it when my car falls into disrepair or stops working, which happens too often, in my opinion.

My first car, a 1972 Mustang, looked sharp with Ford's Grabber Blue color, especially when I replaced the factory tires and hub caps with bigger tires and mag wheels. Unfortunately, the 302-centimeter engine was underpowered, the car rusted like a tin can, and even a little winter precipitation was like driving on an ice rink.

A used 1979 Impala was my second car, and it performed okay until I noticed a grinding noise coming from the right-front wheel area. I stopped to talk to my mechanic, whose shop was next door to my Oconomowoc newspaper office.

"It's not urgent, but I wouldn't drive another 500 miles without having it checked out," he told me.

That evening, I drove six miles down the Interstate to meet a buddy for nighttime cross-country skiing. I was two blocks from home when the wheel came off the spindle. I was stuck in the middle of the street and had to call a wrecker.

My third car was a used Dodge Omni. Late one night, I was driving home to Wisconsin Rapids after picking up my toddler son from his grandparents' home. I had attended the community's Milwaukee Brewers Night at County Stadium. Suddenly, the car stopped running. The alternator was kaput. I hitched a ride with a Good Samaritan who lived where my car died, but, because I got home much later than expected, I was accused of having an affair.

SNAKES, SQUIRRELS & BEARS, OH MY!

My first car was a 1972 Mustang. Ford's Grabber Blue color and my mag wheels made it look sharp, but it was underpowered and rusted terribly.

After getting divorced, I bought a new Plymouth Laser. Like the Mustang, it looked sporty but lacked giddyup. During one cold snap, I let the gas tank get a little low, and the car wouldn't start. It sat for a week on the street outside my Janesville apartment until the weather warmed. Fortunately, I was within walking distance of work.

I traded the Laser for a used Ford Ranger. This pickup's design and purple paint looked nice. The topper and the side-saddle seats in a small extended cab made it a great utility vehicle. But the starter seemed balky, kicking over the engine one time, requiring that I turn the key several times the next. I returned to the dealership and explained the problem. As my salesman listened, a mechanic said it was just that starter and nothing was wrong with it.

Several months later, the starter went out. I returned to the dealer and demanded it be fixed at no charge.

"Gosh, if you'd have returned it immediately, we'd have covered it, but now it's been longer than ninety days."

"I did! Go get my salesman; he'll tell you that I reported the problem right after buying this truck." Steam rolled out of my ears.

The salesman confirmed my claim, and the manager conceded they'd fix the problem.

One day I was driving up Courthouse Hill after work and it suddenly sounded like an airplane was landing on the roof. I wondered what the hell was going on and drove to my mechanic's shop.

"Your four-wheel drive is going out," he said of the system that engaged with a dashboard push-button. "I could replace it with a system where you'd have to get out and turn each hub."

I imagined doing that on the freeway when a winter storm hit, flatlanders and other inconsiderate drivers flying past my backside without moving out of the adjacent lane. Instead, I traded that truck for a new GMC Sonoma and bought a matching red topper.

When, after a couple years, the Sonoma developed a front-end oil leak and GMC offered zero percent financing on new vehicles, I bought an identical Sonoma and moved the topper to it. I hoped that if the leak was inherent, the manufacturer had solved the problem. It proved to be the worst vehicle purchase of my life.

The battery leaked, and the truck developed oil leaks in both the front and back ends. Even worse, the starter—like that in my Ranger—turned fickle. I returned the truck to the dealer for inspection.

"Are you using an aftermarket key in this?" a mechanic said.

"Yes."

"Well, don't use that; there's your problem."

"That makes no sense because I've been using the aftermarket key for months without the starter acting up."

"Well, just don't use it; it lacks the computerization of the factory key."

I left shaking my head. A month later, my first book was back at the publisher, and I left work at noon on a Tuesday and met my parents in Stevens Point to pick up four boxes of books so I could do signings that weekend. The book focused on a tragedy in Portage, and on my way back to Janesville, I stopped to do an interview with the Portage paper. Returning to my truck, I turned the key.

Nothing.

I tried again and again. Nothing.

Back in the newspaper office, I waited awhile, then went out to try the truck again. Nothing. Again and again, nothing.

My second wife, Cheryl, worked in Madison and by then would be home for supper. I called her.

"Hi, Hon, I'm in Portage, and the damn truck won't start. Can you come and pick me up?"

"What? I just drove home from work. Now you want me to turn around and drive to Portage?"

"Yes. I know it's a pain in the butt, but so is this truck. And I have to get back to the office tonight and catch up on work I didn't finish before leaving for the afternoon."

She came and got me.

I was still angry about my plight the next day and called the dealer. "Look, you guys told me the only thing wrong with my starter was that I was using an aftermarket key and to stop doing that. So I did. Now the truck is in Portage, and it won't start. My wife had to drive up and get me last night so I could get back to work. Now you're going to drive a flatbed up there, retrieve the truck, fix the damn starter, and I'm not going to pay a dime for it."

They did, and I didn't.

I'd had enough of GMC and its troubled Sonomas, so I read Consumer Reports and its glowing reports about little sport-utility vehicles from Honda and Toyota. A few days later I called my salesman at the GMC/Honda dealership. "Price me out a Honda CR-V."

I drove a 2008 CR-V and liked it. Before pulling the trigger, however, I also drove Toyota's RAV4. When the Honda dealer gave me a better trade-in value and lower interest rate, the CR-V came home with me.

My wife, a lifelong General Motors owner in a former GM town, wasn't convinced. She thought I'd have problems with a foreign vehicle, so I bought an extended warranty package.

That proved to be a waste of money. The only trouble I had with the CR-V was that it burned out headlights—more than in all other vehicles I'd owned combined. Still, I liked the vehicle's utility functions and gas mileage. Compared to past products, my CR-V was trouble-free.

Nearly 100,000 miles later, however, I could foresee retirement. In 2014, I test-drove the Nissan Rogue, the Mazda CX-5, the Subaru Outback, and the Ford Escape. Buying another Honda was the easy call.

My 2014 CR-V has been a dream. The ride, storage space, and hauling capabilities are significant steps up from the utilitarian ones on the 2008 model. It gets better gas mileage. I even learned that if I remove the front wheel from our tandem bicycle, we can slide the bike inside and take it on trips.

"I've owned lots of different vehicles—Fords, Chevys, Dodges, and Mazdas among them," I told my salesman several years later. "My 2014 CR-V is by far my favorite. It's a great utility vehicle, good on gas, and hasn't had mechanical problems. If I had enough money to buy a second one, I'd do so and store it away until this one is shot."

Still, in 2021, my CR-V rolled past 100,000 miles. During an oil change, I talked to my salesman, now the sales manager. He priced me out a new one.

"What about the interior space in the back end?" I said. "How does it compare to my 2014? We use our tandem bicycle a lot, and I can get it inside with the front wheel off."

"I don't have those numbers off the top of my head," he said. "But you can measure one if you'd like."

I drove up a few days later, tape measure in hand. But when I saw that the center console had a higher profile, I stopped measuring.

"Is that the only option on the console?" I asked the sales manager.

"Yes."

"Well, then I guess I'm going to keep this one for now. I like being able to haul our tandem bicycle in it."

I'm confident that my 2014 CR-V will roll past 200,000 miles, maybe while that bike is tucked inside.

But given my troubled history with cars, I still fear that any day now you'll find me stranded along the side of some road.

27
When the IRS Wants a Chunk of You

The year: 2011.

The date: Notice dated September 12, 2011, months after Cheryl and I received and cashed a substantial income tax refund after filing our *2010* income tax returns.

The trouble: A letter from the Internal Revenue Service.

Driving home on a Friday night from my job as Opinion Page editor of *The Janesville Gazette*, I anticipated a nice dinner with Cheryl and our friends from New Berlin. The first thing I did upon arriving was check the mail.

Big mistake. Among a fistful of letters was one from the IRS. Never a good thing.

Opening it ruined our evening. It suggested we owed $17,205 in extra taxes, penalties, and interest not from 2010 but *2009*.

I had been relying on a former colleague as my tax preparer. Each year I tried to provide every possible bit of information, and each year Tax Guy called with questions. But 2009 had been particularly troublesome. Having changed all our mutual fund holdings from a national investment company to oversight through BMO Harris Bank meant that, instead of the one pile of statements, we had two piles to sort out.

This dual avalanche of paperwork apparently left Tax Guy confused about which were "qualified" retirement accounts and which were "nonqualified" accounts. The IRS letter stated we still owed taxes on some $56,000 of "unclaimed income."

The document stated, "The income and payment information (e.g., wages, miscellaneous income, interest, income tax withheld, earned income credit, etc.) that we have on file does not match entries on your 2009 Form 1040. If this information is correct, you will owe $17,205."

Under "Summary of Proposed Changes," it put our 2009 tax increase at $13,541, penalties of $2,708 and interest, "if paid by October 12, 2011," of $956.

Ugh.

"How did this happen," I fumed, "and where are we gonna find more than $17,000 to pay the IRS?"

I was anything but pleasant company that night. I even interrupted our evening to call Tax Guy.

"Send me a copy of the letter, and all of your statements again," he said.

I stewed the rest of the night and slept fitfully for days afterward, while Tax Guy sorted out the mess, called me repeatedly with questions, and prepared amended returns.

While those days were full of stress, it turns out that I had no need to fret. My subsequent letter to an agent at the IRS Service Center in Cincinnati, along with our amended returns, stated:

"Enclosed is our response to your letter suggesting we owed taxes on some $56,000 of 'unclaimed income' on our 2009 tax returns. Those numbers did not take into account the cost basis for those investments, so they also did not factor in the losses. Please see the enclosed amended returns."

The result: Instead of us paying $17,205, the amended returns suggested Uncle Sam actually owed *us* $1,091.

Of course, I had to pay Tax Guy $210 out of that for his extra work.

The IRS agent reviewed our letter and amended returns and concurred.

Though the whole ordeal probably shaved a year or two off my life, we were delighted to cash that extra check!

28
Six Things That Could Go Wrong When Remodeling (Your Results May Vary)

"Don, I've got a problem. Call me as soon as you can."

With the help of Don Hoch, a handy buddy and former coworker, I planned to remodel the basement bathroom in our 1940s Janesville home.

The project seemed easy enough. As a teenager, I worked for a Dutchman who built homes while wearing wooden shoes. This meticulous craftsman had me doing mostly grunt work.

"Where's your eagle eye?" he'd chastise me when I missed a nail and hammered dents into a deck board.

I do know my way around a hammer and saw. Still, I hired Don to help me with this project. I figured the job might consume three days. We were only replacing the shower stall, the drop ceiling, and the carpeting. The sink, two vanities, and toilet would stay. A fresh coat of paint would complete the new look. What could go wrong?

Turns out, plenty. Even before Don arrived, I'd run into a problem, one of six we'd encounter.

1. Getting said stall in the basement.

Janesville has two leading big-box building materials stores. I favor Menards over Home Depot because I struggle to find a warm body to help me at the Depot. So Cheryl and I visited Menards to inspect their shower stalls. Unfortunately, most had the drain 12 inches from the corner, while the drain in the floor of our old 36-inch shower stall was centered. Menards could order one with a centered drain, but shipping would take a month and I couldn't be certain of a proper fit.

Home Depot had two sizes of one model with a centered drain. Both were in two pieces. The bottom piece included the floor and the first third of the three side walls. The top piece was shaped like a large square-cornered "C." I wasn't sure our stairway was wide enough. So we drove home to measure before buying.

It wasn't even a close fit. Our basement stairway is 32 inches wide, but a second stairway leads to our basement from the garage. Trouble is, we hadn't used that door in a decade. Weather-stripping sealed it shut. In the garage, the stairwell housed three ladders, the snowblower, and garden tools and ornaments. The back hallway leading to that door in the basement stored my fishing equipment, boxes of Christmas stuff, and more garden ornaments.

Still, to get the larger unit in the basement, clearing that stairwell and prying open that door seemed like the best bet.

We returned to Home Depot, bought the $450 shower stall, rented a truck, and toted the unit home.

I managed to clear the stored stuff, then lowered the top portion of the shower into the stairwell just outside the doorway. It was a tight squeeze. A Home Depot staffer said something about a little flexibility, so I thought I could bend it a tad and squeeze it through.

Bad idea. I was nearly sick to my stomach when one corner cracked.

I left the unit sit in the stairwell and gave Cheryl the bad news when she returned home from shopping.

"Why didn't you wait for Don to help you?" she chastised.

"It was so close, I thought it would fit," I said, walking away and mumbling something about hindsight being 20-20.

That night, I slept fitfully.

The next day, prompted by my frantic phone call, Don arrived.

"Oh, that's not such a bad crack," he suggested, much to my relief. "We should be able to caulk it, and because it's on the top, no one will notice it."

Still, the shower stall wasn't yet in the house. Don attacked one door jamb with his Sawzall to give us room to get the unit inside.

What a battle. Turns out, that jamb was not just nailed to the concrete foundation but bolted. He spent an hour cutting and prying and splintering that stubborn plank before wrestling it out of there.

The shower stall slipped into the basement without further damage.

With the door to the bathroom removed, the big unit fit into the intended space. Its drain hole and the floor's drain also matched. That's good because, what with that crack, I couldn't return the unit.

2. Don't sit there just yet!

But the second day, I noticed the handle to the toilet was askew. We must have bumped it while grappling with the shower stall. A gander inside the toilet tank revealed that we broke the shaft behind the handle. Because the toilet had interior workings akin to something you'd see in an antiques shop, we had to buy a kit and cobble together new and old parts.

A modest fix, both in terms of cost and time.

Please resume flushing.

3. Hazard ahead.

Don and I also removed the drop ceiling, with rusting crossbars and yellowing panels, that first day. On Day 3, Don stopped over and expressed concern over the now-exposed asbestos-wrapped pipes above us.

"You know, that asbestos wrapping is frayed. Some of those fibers are likely falling on us. If you were ever gonna get that stuff removed, now'd be the time, with the ceiling out."

I couldn't disagree. Knowing the asbestos was up there, on pipes tied to our boiler furnace, always troubled me.

I grabbed the phone book. The Yellow Pages listed just one company, JD Environmental of Delavan, under "asbestos removal." I told Don I'd try calling, but I wondered how much the task might set me back.

"Probably $600 or $700," he guessed.

I was thinking even more.

"Who knows when they might be able to get a crew here?" I told Cheryl. "It might be three or four weeks for all I know."

She has never accused me of being an optimist.

In late afternoon, on my second try, I got ahold of the right guy, Jamie. I described the pipes, and he suggested I email a photo and he could quote me a price by phone.

I did so. The next morning came a glimmer of good news.

"It looks like $300," he said.

I stifled a gleeful response.

"And," Jamie followed with even brighter news, "we have a crew over working in Janesville right now. I could have someone over there tomorrow afternoon."

Before I could respond, he went one better.

"Wait, I could have someone over there at 1 o'clock."

"We'll be here!" I said with excessive exuberance.

With the asbestos gone, Don and I were back at it the next day.

4. What do you mean I can't drive that truck?

We needed two sheets of wallboard. Cheryl and I returned to Menards on a soggy day to buy the wallboard and rent a truck to haul it. The forecasted rains had paused, and I hoped to get the wallboards home before they got wet. In case rain reoccurred, I had boards along to keep the wallboards out of the damp truck bed and a tarp to wrap over them.

Having bought a new grill and rented this truck a month earlier, I knew the routine. Show driver's license and insurance card, sign to rent truck.

But wait!

"I can't let you drive the truck," the attendant said.

"Why not?"

"Because your wife's name is on the insurance card, but not yours. She will have to drive."

"But she doesn't even have her purse and driver's license! Are you telling me we have to drive home to get her purse just to rent the truck?"

"Yes, sorry."

"Wait! I rented this truck a month ago using the same insurance card, and you were the person who let me drive it!"

"Sorry, I can't let you drive it."

I thought about all the purchases I'd made at Menards since retiring three months earlier. Menards had become like my second home.

I was furious.

We raced home, me stomping on the gas pedal at every opportunity, after every stoplight, and cursing all the way. I wondered how my wife, all of 5-foot-2, could reach the gas pedal in that monstrous Ford pickup.

On the way back to Menards, it struck me. The insurance card has the insurance agent's phone number. Couldn't Menards just call to confirm that I'm insured, too?

When we arrived at the counter, I posed that idea.

"You can call," the attendant said, and I asked to use their phone. "Have them fax the proof of insurance to this number."

Ten minutes later, I was driving the big truck. Somehow, we managed to get the wallboards home before it rained again.

The wallboards went up, Don did a good job "mudding" the new walls, and we were ready for painting. I applied two coats in a single day.

Next came installing the new ceiling. It wasn't an easy task because that part of the ceiling slanted to expose a glass-block window. My new paint job got dinged up, requiring touchups. In one spot, Don tried tacking the trim rail, only to hammer through the wallboard, leaving a small hole to mud and paint over.

5. No so fan-tastic.

On Wednesday of Week 2, the end was in sight. "We might finish today or tonight if we can only get this ceiling fan hooked up again," I said.

"That won't be a problem," Don replied.

Famous last words.

The fan had a timer, and Don hooked it up, but nothing happened. He tested and retested, once or twice getting a jolt as I repeatedly asked if he wanted me to flip the circuit breaker.

Finally, after an hour of fiddling, wiring, and rewiring, he gave up.

"You'll have to call an electrician," he said.

Don left, and I started calling.

The first couldn't come before Tuesday. The second had just an answering machine, so I hung up.

The third, Westphal Electric, scheduled an appointment for first thing Monday.

6. The final meltdown.

On Friday, I was back at Menards for two reasons. First, I had a few leftover materials to return. Second, I needed a new hose for my ShopVac.

I had been caulking around the new shower, using a high-intensity utility light to illuminate the task. Seems I wasn't paying attention to where my vacuum was, and the hot lamp melted the hose right to it. The refund on the materials I returned to Menards *almost* covered the new hose kit.

I got back in the car and noticed Cheryl had tried reaching me on my cell phone. Westphal had a guy available right away, and she told him to come over but wasn't sure what the project entailed. I called back, said I was on my way, and raced home.

He was already there. I explained the situation, and he soon determined the timer was shot. Replacing it might delay the fix and cost more money. He suggested removing it and adding a separate switch for the fan.

"That'd be fine," I said.

An hour and $100 later, the fan was humming.

Cheryl planned to visit a craft fair with her friends that Saturday, and I was confident I could finish placing the two panels under the fluorescent ceiling light, install the carpet, touch up blemishes on the new paint job, and rehang two towel bars and the door with a new stopper before she got home.

I did so, and even had time to vacuum—with my new hose—and put away the tools and store salvageable scrap materials.

I called Don and invited him to come and inspect the final product. He and his wife, Barb, were marveling at the finished look when Cheryl arrived.

She, too, was impressed.

This project took three times as long as I figured and cost twice my initial hoped-for $1,000, but the asbestos was out, everything looked fresh and new, and I was ready to get out of Cheryl's hair and her upstairs bathroom.

No doubt, you've heard experienced do-it-yourselfers suggest you'll run into pitfalls regardless of what project you tackle. Trust me—those people know what they're talking about.

29
The Tale of Todd

Todd doesn't come out to play anymore.

That's because I've found a new partner, a new friend. This one is better looking and isn't as heavyset.

Todd and I became competitive partners years ago. I don't recall the exact year when we became teammates. It was decades ago.

I do know that I wasn't Todd's first teammate. I never met Todd's first partner.

But, odd as it might seem, his name was Todd, too. Somewhere along the line, for reasons I'll never know, they split. I'm sure Todd would have felt used, if Todd had felt anything at all.

When I first picked up Todd as my partner, we didn't quite mesh; we weren't a good fit. I wanted Todd to change a bit, and Todd did.

Working together, we started out slowly. Each time we competed, Todd was right there, helping me as we worked side by side. Little by little, I gained confidence in my abilities, our abilities. I believed that someday we could achieve great things together.

Then, one autumn evening, it happened. Todd and I got on a roll and reached for glory. I know the exact date—it was Oct. 8, 2000.

We were nearly flawless. People all around us stopped what they were doing to watch us. Those who knew us well were amazed because Todd and I never showed that much promise before.

But, at the last moment, we blew it. It really wasn't Todd's fault. I don't blame Todd at all. I was the one who failed us. My emotions, my nerves, got the best of me.

Still, our achievement made the newspaper. I worked for the paper, and I was so enamored with our accomplishment that I wrote a story that explained how we did it and what it felt like.

Todd and I would never come close to that special moment again. Maybe that, too, was my fault. Maybe I got a big head. Maybe I thought I was somehow suddenly better than Todd.

I became frustrated at our failings.

In the months that followed, I started to think about finding a new partner. A couple of years later, I did. I abandoned Todd.

Oh, we competed together off and on for another year or two. But those times became fewer and fewer as I worked with my new partner. Todd hasn't joined me in competition now for years.

It's sad, really. That's especially so because my new partner and I haven't been all that great together. We've never come close to that one shining moment when Todd and I basked in near glory.

Todd is there, though, when I compete these days. But Todd doesn't watch me. Todd can't watch me.

Todd stays tucked away, in a bag built for two, and I'm left with little but fond memories of my old partner, my bowling ball named Todd.

30
Everything Came Up Roses

"Are you sure you've got tickets to the game?"

"Yes, Dad," I said. "It's a package deal. Game tickets are part of the deal."

It was late December, 1993. Cheryl and I had been dating for a year and saving money to vacation in Jamaica. However, the Badger football team had ascended in four short years under coach Barry Alvarez and made the Rose Bowl for the first time since 1963. I had no thoughts about going until I spotted an ad in the Milwaukee paper. It pitched a package that included flight to Los Angeles, hotel, and tickets to enjoy not only the game but also the Rose Bowl Parade and Universal Studios. All ground transportation was included. The price? About $850.

"Honey, check out this ad. Whaddya say we spend our Jamaica money on the Rose Bowl?"

I didn't expect much enthusiasm.

"Yes!" she said with a big smile.

Wow, I thought. This one's a keeper! Using our savings for that planned island vacation, we called and booked the California trip.

Soon, news reports emerged about a ticket scandal. Tour operators were pitching packages that included game tickets, but for many such companies, who expected to pay the usual rate of about $150 a pop to brokers, those tickets weren't in hand.

I remained confident despite those reports.

"Stop worrying," I told Dad repeatedly.

Turns out, Dad had plenty of reason to fret.

As a follow-up story by the *Los Angeles Times* reported, 60,000 Badger fans had designs on seeing that game. "They started a run on tickets unlike anything Pasadena had ever seen."

Desperate Badger backers paid scalpers up to $600 per seat. Still, hundreds more never stepped inside the Rose Bowl. Many blamed UCLA, which was allotted twice as many tickets as Wisconsin. Then UCLA sold a block to a booster, who resold them to a broker, who charged Badger fans as much as 10 times face value, according to the *LA Times*.

Cheryl and I flew to Los Angeles a couple of days early. Our tour of Universal Studios came the day before the big game. A sea of red filled our hotel lobby as the tour operator shouted out names for our theme park tickets. When our names were called, we climbed aboard one of three buses spewing diesel fumes.

Meeting a Lucille Ball lookalike was part of our Universal Studios tour a day before the Rose Bowl game.

"I'd like to know why they didn't just hand out tickets to the parade and game at the same time," I said to Cheryl.

She had no good answer, and that question puzzled me throughout our enjoyable day at the film studios, where we photographed the clock tower used in a favorite film "Back to the Future," witnessed an old wild west shootout, and I posed for a snapshot with a Lucille Ball lookalike.

When we got back to the hotel, I visited the desk clerk.

"Do you have any idea why the tour company didn't hand out tickets to the game this morning rather than create another crush of humanity in your lobby tomorrow morning?"

A float featuring a massive genie passes our viewing area during the Rose Bowl Parade. Unfortunately, a building next to our assigned bleacher seats blocked our view of floats as they approached, but we were just happy to be witnessing the parade.

The clerk leaned toward me, glanced around to make sure no one else could hear him, and said: "Word has it that they're going through the UCLA dorms right now, trying to buy tickets."

I shuddered. "What!?"

"They don't have enough tickets for everybody," he continued. "They're trying to buy them from UCLA students."

Cheryl and I were dumbstruck, and I felt light-headed.

"I need a drink," I said, and we stumbled in shock toward the hotel bar. "Guess Dad was right to be concerned."

Adding insult to injury, I ordered a brandy old-fashioned. It would be my first lesson in the idea that bartenders on our nation's coasts couldn't make a drinkable old-fashioned if their game tickets depended on it.

Later, back in our room, I didn't dare dial Dad and further distress him with an update. Sleep didn't come easily that night. My nerves were frazzled the next morning as we again stepped into that red sea in the lobby where we waited, holding our breath, to hear our names.

Finally, after what seemed an excruciatingly torturous delay, our names were called. Cheryl and I gripped our parade and game tickets as we climbed aboard the bus, smiles of relief on our faces.

The parade tickets had a face value of $28 apiece for bleacher seats furnished by Sharp Seating Company. Our tickets to the 80th Rose Bowl, face value $46, were for seats 108 and 109 in Row 11, Tunnel 6. They gave no indication that we'd be seated among a mass of UCLA Bruin students clad in blue and gold.

Had we not gotten tickets to the game, my disposition would have matched that of this fierce dragon on a parade float.

The bus made an arduous journey through bumper-to-bumper traffic snaking along streets to Pasadena and the spot where we could unload and climb to our bleacher seats. The snarl took so long that the parade had already started when we finally poured out.

Only then did we learn that our seats were *on the other side of the street*, and a traffic cop wouldn't let us cross. As soon as he looked the other way, however, our bus mates started bolting, and we joined them, scurrying across. Thankfully, no one got arrested.

Wearing our Badger red Rose Bowl sweatshirts, we reached our seats high in the bleachers before the first float drifted past. Sitting in mostly sunny skies with temperatures around 70, we chuckled thinking about the weather back home, where another Wisconsin winter was in full swing.

We enjoyed the many beautiful floats, including those with a tall dragon, a long pink dinosaur, and the Disneyland one featuring Mickey

Cheryl, sporting black slacks to the left, poses for a photo outside the famous Rose Bowl stadium.

Mouse. However, a building next to the bleachers obscured the approaching floats; each was right in front of us before we had a good view.

Then it was back on the bus and on to the game. We snapped photos outside the iconic stadium, and as soon as we found our spots and sat down, four male UCLA students stood up in the row behind us and started chanting, "Take off those red shirts. Take off those red shirts."

We laughed, and they seemed ready for a good time. I gazed around us, and while red dots were sprinkled among the blue in this UCLA student section, we were isolated from other Badger fans. When UCLA kicked a field goal to grab the lead, these four students nudged us, demanding we be good sports and give them high fives. We played along.

But when Brent Moss plowed in from three yards out to give the Badgers the lead later in the first quarter, the four ignored us. We

SNAKES, SQUIRRELS & BEARS, OH MY!

Badger quarterback Darrell Bevell had a clean pocket for passing on this play. Bevell later scampered for the decisive touchdown.

playfully elbowed them and held up our hands, but when we glanced back, they looked elsewhere.

These fellows seemed even cooler toward us when Moss scored again in the second quarter, and halftime approached with the Badgers holding a comfortable 14-3 lead.

"Wait until you see our marching band," one of the four chortled. "They're the best."

"If you say so," I said. "But the Badgers have a pretty good marching band, too."

When UCLA's band took the field, I was underwhelmed. Their music seemed quiet compared to the raucous tunes the Badger band was known for. After both groups had performed, these four students admitted that, yes, the UW band is impressive.

Neither team scored in the third quarter, but it worried me when two players from each team were ejected after a fight. Among them was UW's top receiver, Lee DeRamus. I wondered how our offense would keep clicking without this pass-catching threat.

When UCLA rushed for a touchdown early in the fourth quarter, closing the gap to 14-10 and again requiring us to high five the guys behind us, Cheryl and I got nervous. Especially with UCLA's top receiver, J.J. Stokes, catching most every ball thrown his way.

But then UW's slow-footed quarterback Darrell Bevell rumbled around the left side of the line and seemingly took an eternity to run 21 yards for a touchdown. UCLA answered with another touchdown to pull within 21-16. The Bruins were driving again in the final minute when their quarterback scrambled rather than throwing the ball away. He got just three yards, to UW's 15-yard line, and time expired before UCLA could again snap the ball.

It marked UW's first Rose Bowl victory in four tries. Stokes had set a Rose Bowl record with 14 catches for 176 yards. However, Moss was named most valuable player after rolling up 158 yards in 36 carries, including those two touchdowns.

Fans dressed in red went crazy, cheering, dancing, and unleashing decades of pent-up frustrations, while our four fair-weather "buddies" behind us made a solemn stroll to the exits.

More celebrating among fellow Badger fans was in store back at the hotel that night. The next morning, before catching a late-afternoon flight home, Cheryl and I rented a car and drove up the Malibu coast, dipping our toes in the chilly Pacific waters.

We arrived home after dark to a foot of unplowed snow in our driveway. And we later learned that a coworker, who graduated from UW, had traveled on a UW Alumni Association package, missed the parade so he could buy high-priced game tickets with cash from a scalper outside the stadium, and then—in the era before people used credit cards like ready cash—was reimbursed *on a credit card*.

From time to time in the years since, the Badgers have returned to the Rose Bowl, including back-to-back victories—a first for any Big Ten team—in 1999 and 2000. Each time, Cheryl has hinted that we should make another trip to the West Coast. But I always tell her that our 1994 Rose Bowl journey was so thrilling, so historic, that going again would dampen those wonderful memories.

31
Children's Heavy Equipment Exhausts Grandparents

It's 8:50 a.m. in late October, 2009, and I'm sitting on the cold driveway, trying to figure out the trick that disengages the bottom tray from The World's Most Elaborate Car Safety Seat.

Waiting in the house, getting impatient, are Grandma and 9-month-old Jeremy, or Remy, as we call him. Remy has been walking for only a few weeks, yet is already The Kid of Perpetual Motion.

Remy's big sister, Lexi, now nearly 8, is trying to help "Papa," as she calls me, with the complicated apparatus. We find one button that disengages half of the bottom, but we can't find the other one. The Spanish words on one side aren't helping, and neither are the English words on the other side. These only explain safety precautions.

We give up, and I wrestle the seat into my small sport-utility vehicle. I discover that it's too long to fit behind my driver's seat.

"We usually put it in the middle," Lexi advises me.

I strap it in there after struggling to get a seat belt with a shoulder strap threaded between the top and bottom of the safety seat. I start strapping in Remy with shoulder and waist harnesses, though with his sweatshirt and jacket, the tot is a tight fit.

Grandma continues the harnessing task as I refocus on The World's Most Elaborate Stroller. I got it to pop up; now I'm trying to figure out how to get it to refold so it fits in the back of said SUV.

"Get our little stroller downstairs," Grandma says.

I mumble something about wishing I'd been home from work when their dad dropped off the kids so I could have asked for a tutorial on the heavy equipment.

Suddenly, I get it—push the button *and* twist the handle at the same time, and The World's Most Elaborate Stroller collapses and is ready for stowing in my SUV.

Remy finally secured, the rest of us jump in, ready to head downtown to the last Janesville Farmers Market of the season. I start the vehicle and begin to back out before it dawns on me.

"Do you have your booster seat?" I ask Big Sister.

Lexi, who legally needs a booster seat until she's 8, even though she's nearly as tall as Grandma, has buckled herself in without asking about the missing booster seat.

I stop, open the garage door, retrieve the booster seat, and suddenly sympathize with our daughter-in-law, who can't seem to leave the house without one more trip inside for a bottle or diaper, sunglasses or cell phone.

As Big Sister buckles herself into the booster seat, I notice that Grandma missed the crotch clasp on The Kid of Perpetual Motion. I dig under a tiny butt, find said clasp, and wrench it into place until I hear that familiar click.

We head down the street, and I think about the instructional schedule their father left with us.

"Remy was supposed to be in bed by 9, and it was 10," I say.

"Uh huh," Grandma says.

"We didn't get Remy up until 8, and he was supposed to be up at 7."

"Yes."

"Now it's 9, and we're supposed to be putting him down for a two-hour nap, and here we are headed for the farmers market."

"Uh huh."

"This could be our last rodeo."

"You might be right."

Meanwhile, in the back seat, The World's Most Elaborate Car Safety Seat is chiming out "How Much Is that Doggie in the Window?"

"I'm not sure about the kids, but I think *we* are gonna need that nap," I say to Grandma.

"Uh huh."

32
Lesson in Liquid Propane

My father grew up on a farm, where he learned to fix everything from an electric fence to a balky tractor. During his work life, he pumped gas, fixed flats, and changed oil and spark plugs at a service station when he wasn't driving a meat truck or installing telephones.

It was Tom, however, the middle of us three brothers, who inherited Dad's knack for tinkering. Tom was schooled in auto body and has repainted classic cars and pulled engines.

In contrast, I've never changed the oil or an air filter on my cars. If I visit an auto parts store to buy a new battery or wiper blades, I ask employees to install them before I drive away.

So it wasn't surprising when I came upon a mechanical problem one warm November day and had no clue what to do. It was such a beautiful stretch of late-autumn weather that Cheryl and I planned on hiking in a county park. We ate lunch before I opened the garage to back my vehicle out.

I had been catching whiffs of liquid propane for several days, not long after getting the spare LP tank for our grill refilled. When I first noticed this offensive smell, I checked the twist valves on both the spare tank and the one on the grill to make sure they were snug. They appeared to be.

Now, however, the stench was stronger than ever, heightening my concern. I went over to the full spare tank, which was sitting next to a window but in shade on a heavy-duty shelf. I reached up and put my hand in front of the valve and was startled to feel gas escaping.

Oh my God, I thought. I scrambled to pull the heavy tank off the shelf, which sits above an open stairwell to our basement. Spewing a string of profanities, I carried the tank outside and set it in the driveway before opening the second garage door to let the foul air dissipate.

"It figures," I complained to Cheryl in even more colorful language. "Try to have some fun while the weather's nice, and all of a sudden I've got a problem to solve."

What to do? I called the propane company and got a recording, then punched "one" for "yes" when it asked if this was an emergency.

A woman answered but seemed clueless about what to do, so she put me on hold until another woman in the company's emergency service responded.

"I've got an LP tank that's leaking at the valve stem," I said. "I just had it refilled at your company a few days ago."

I glanced down at the tank and was shocked to see frost coating the metal around the valve.

"Now the valve is turning white from the escaping gas," I told her. "What should I do?"

"Do you have a truck?"

"No."

"Well, ideally, you would put it in the back of a truck and drive it to our shop to have it inspected."

"What if I put it in the back of my SUV and drove with all the windows down?" I imagined that the three-mile drive, with windows down, wouldn't cause me to pass out.

"I can't advise that," she said. "You should call and talk to your local fire department for advice."

I hung up and thought of two neighbors with pickup trucks. I could see that one wasn't home because he always parked in his driveway. I ran across the street and punched the doorbell at the other home, thinking the truck might be in his garage.

No one responded.

I hurried home and dialed 757-2244, my county's nonemergency number, which was drummed into my head through a country musician's promotional commercial song. Still, the last thing I needed was fire trucks, sirens blaring, racing to a stop at my house so the neighbors would come running and rubbernecking while wondering what the hell was going on.

A dispatcher advised me to call the fire lieutenant on duty at Station One. He gave me the number, and I dialed it.

Instead of getting the lieutenant, I got his voice mail. I hung up without leaving a message.

Time was slipping away. If Cheryl and I were to still enjoy our hike, I had to solve this problem soon. I decided to risk it.

Rather than put the tank in the back of my SUV, where the smell likely would still be strong even with the windows rolled down, I backed Cheryl's four-door Chevy out of the garage, rolled down all the windows, and tossed the tank in the trunk.

"I'm off," I told her. "Wish me luck."

I pushed the speed limit as much as I dared as I raced through the city and swerved around trucks entering and exiting an industrial district. But I got stuck behind a lumbering dump truck as we reached a rural stoplight with both of us planning left turns.

I waited impatiently, thinking about the leaking tank in the trunk behind me and wishing I had rocketed around the dump truck before reaching the intersection. When the light turned green, I creeped ahead to look past the truck for oncoming traffic as the driver started his turn. The path seemed clear, so I snugged up behind the truck.

That's when the trucker, apparently a greenhorn driver, started grinding gears. His hulking truck almost stalled midturn. I was stuck in the oncoming traffic lane as a big SUV barreled toward me.

Flashing before my eyes was the scene of a collision ripping open the LP tank and triggering a deadly explosion.

"Local Author Perishes in Fiery Blast Triggered by Faulty LP Tank," the headline would read.

But somehow, some way, the dump truck cleared the intersection, and I slipped in behind it, avoiding the approaching SUV.

In another half mile, I reached the LP company and rolled up to the elevated service garage. I scrambled out as the male attendant came to the doorway to greet me.

"I have a leaking tank," I told him breathlessly. "One of your guys filled it a few days ago. I haven't used it, but I've been smelling gas in the garage since then."

"I see," the man said. "Lemme have a look."

He bent over to grab the handle of the tank as I hoisted it up to him.

"Maybe it's a little too full," he said. He used a tool to let a small cloud of white gas escape. He took it out a side door of the garage and let out more gas. Back inside, he put it on the filling machine and tested the level.

"That should do it," he said.

"So what was the problem?"

"Well, the guy maybe filled it a little too full. Warm weather like this makes the gas expand, and these tanks have a little overfill valve that lets some escape if there's too much gas."

"Oh," I said, embarrassed at my cluelessness. "That's nice."

"Sorry," he said.

"That's okay," I said. "I'm just glad it wasn't anything serious."

I placed the tank back in Cheryl's trunk and, as I drove home, it dawned on me: I had filled the tank on a day with freezing temperatures. With this day's unseasonably warm weather surging toward 60, it was no wonder the tank was releasing extra pressure. It was designed that way.

Glad that this apparent crisis was behind me, I checked the dashboard clock. We still had time to take that hike.

As we walked, I realized that afternoon's lesson was one more step in lessening my mechanical ignorance.

33
Walks to Remember

It wasn't there the morning before, and it didn't look like it belonged. What was it?

Only when Trapper, our cairn terrier, and I got closer could I tell for sure. It was a section of someone's white picket fence. Seems that the previous night some driver—probably after a few too many drinks—had careened into a front yard on Janesville's east side, clipped a fence and dragged the chunk down the sidewalk, leaving skid marks before depositing the damaged pickets against a big ash tree. Trapper let out a little woof and stopped to sniff the out-of-place fence.

It was just one of many odd scenes I came across on daily mile-long strolls across the past two decades with first Trapper, then Molly.

There was the time a handful of loaded shotgun shells lay along a curb line. Not knowing whether there might have been some overnight shootout, and not wanting them to fall into the hands of curious neighbor kids, I called the police.

A lost cell phone and scattered contents of a wallet or purse—likely from thieves riffling through unlocked cars and tossing items of no use to them—also went to the police station.

Plenty of birds crossed our path. Turkey vultures sat high in tall pines, drying their wings in the morning sunlight. A flock of cedar waxwings ravaged a serviceberry tree for two days before moving on for its next feast. One morning, a Cooper's Hawk flew into a tree as Molly and I approached, and it sat eating its victim as we passed a few feet below it.

Once, Molly and I came to an intersection and someone had placed a stuffed bunny on a stop sign post. I suspected the homeowner had found it and used its long, floppy ears to tie it to the post two feet off the ground, where the family that lost it might spot it. It stayed there a week before disappearing as quickly as it had appeared.

Perhaps more entertaining—at least in my eyes—was the time an attractive, young coworker, a new bride, came scampering out to the curb in her skimpy yellow nightie, ignoring our approach, to give her hubby a goodbye kiss.

The oddest thing, however, was the time Trapper and I stepped out and found pots and pans and their lids sprinkled across our side yard. It was as if giant metal mushrooms had sprouted in the early-morning dew.

As Trapper sniffed them, I gathered them up—more than two dozen in all—before we proceeded on our walk. I could only guess that someone had raided a box of rummage sale items left outside overnight.

But who chose to plant them in our yard, and why?

Those are two answers that Trapper and I never sniffed out.

34
Don't Fall for It

Our exercise instructor passed out an informational pamphlet about avoiding falls at home. The tips included such things as proper lighting, installing grab bars in your bath or shower, and discarding throw rugs because they're trip hazards.

Standing in a sea of older people at the athletic club, I chuckled. I might have been the youngest person there.

Yet coincidentally, two of my favorite elderly ladies in the class had been conspicuously absent for several weeks, only to return with harrowing stories of how they fell on ice and suffered broken bones and bruises. I sympathized.

My immediate reaction was that I didn't need to consider these tips. But obviously, some of those attending these classes, alternating between cardio-fitness and senior yoga each weekday, sure needed them.

Granted, falls are no laughing matter. But then I started thinking back.

Our garage has a stairwell to the basement. When I moved in, a set of railings helped prevent accidental falls into the L-shaped stairwell. However, I'd removed the short piece blocking the first few steps so I could park my lawn mower there, the handle extending where that section of railing was anchored. I figured, what could be the harm? Besides, we only used the stairwell to store ladders, the snowblower or mower—depending on the season—and other seasonal items.

One day I moved the mower and was about to place an electric pole saw back on its hook adjacent to the stairway. As I was looking up at the hook, I stepped right into the gap of that first step.

Planter pots and a wash tub tumbled down the stairs as I plunged into the abyss. Instinctively, I reached out for the sturdy, built-in shelf above the stairwell, catching my fall at the last second.

Brushing myself off, I surveyed the damage to planters now lying at the base of the stairwell. I shuddered. I considered the sharp edge of unforgiving concrete that my head might have smacked had I not grabbed that shelf.

Cheryl was inside. I wondered whether she hadn't heard the banging and crashing. I stepped inside to see why she hadn't come to check on the source of the commotion.

"Hi, Hon," I said cheerfully. "Hear any noise out there?"

"Yes. What happened?"

"I almost fell into the damned stairwell. A bunch of pots and other stuff crashed to the bottom."

"Oh," she said without much alarm, adding, "Are you okay?"

"I grabbed the shelf above the stairwell to stop my fall. Had I missed it, how long would you have waited before finding my crumpled body at the bottom?"

She had no good answer, and I returned to my garage chores while mumbling to myself. It was a good lesson: Be more careful around those steps.

That wasn't my only close call. Far from it. I've found that even walking our dog can pose danger.

One time, Molly and I were several blocks from home. A light dusting of snow had covered a patch of ice over a sunken slab of sidewalk. Molly and I were cruising along when I hit that spot. It was like slipping on sawdust covering an old-time dance floor.

I wound up on my back, cursing the homeowners for ignoring the hazard and cursing myself for not remembering that low spot and being cautious. I scrambled to my feet in anger. I knew an older couple lived there. Ringing their doorbell, I asked the man if he was aware of the treacherous sidewalk in front of his home.

"Do you have any sand or salt?" I asked.

"Yes."

"Good," I said. "If you didn't, I was gonna bring some over to toss down."

Other than a sore back, I walked away unscathed.

Such wasn't the case one Christmas morning. Cheryl's son Adam and his family were visiting for the holiday, and they'd brought their little terrier mix, Ollie. I noticed a freezing drizzle had fallen overnight, so I stepped cautiously out the door, Molly on one leash, Ollie on another. I had failed to strap my ice grips to my hiking shoes, and the sloped driveway was slippery, so I made my way to the grass to reach the level sidewalk. That was icy, too, but I thought the salt and passing of cars on the street might have made that better for walking.

It wasn't much better, so I returned to the sidewalk, stepping carefully. I was almost back, just one long block from home, feeling confident, thinking about the day's holiday activities—church, meals, gift openings—instead of watching my step.

As I reached the sidewalk ramp at a street corner, the slight but icy slope sent me flying. I slammed hard on my lower back and left hip, losing the grip on Ollie's leash. My tumble and scream of pain must have scared Ollie, who dashed across the street. I was glad no cars were coming.

My first thought was that I'd fractured my hip, at least cracked the bone. The pain was excruciating. Somehow, using sheer will, I struggled to my feet, calling Ollie as I did. He returned reluctantly, and I managed to grab his leash.

Doubting I could walk, I slowly took one step, then two. The pain was almost unbearable. Tears filled my eyes. I took a few more steps before a car approached. I thought about flagging down the driver to tell him I needed a ride home or to please stop at my house and summon my relatives.

But I let him pass. Slowly, painfully, surely, I inched my way home, redoubling my caution on the treacherous walkways. What should have taken three minutes took fifteen.

I got to the door, let the dogs run inside ahead of me, and managed to climb the two steps to the threshold by gripping the door jamb with both hands.

"Cheryl," I cried out. "I need help."

Sensing the anguish in my voice, she came running.

"I fell on the ice," I said. "I might have cracked my hip bone."

Cheryl helped me to my recliner, then got me some Tylenol. Tears kept coming amid the pain. Church was out of the question. There I sat the rest of the day, moving only to inch myself to the bathroom. My pain put a damper on our holiday festivities.

That night, after several rounds of pain pills and gripping the handrail with all my might, I managed to climb the stairs to our bedroom. I slept fitfully, but the next day I felt a bit better. Maybe I'd only strained my hip rather than fractured or cracked it, I reasoned.

Still, I couldn't walk Molly. The third day, I managed to walk around the outside of the house. A day later, with Adam's family back home in Illinois, I walked Molly around the block. Little by little, I gained strength until we returned to our walk of nearly a mile.

The pain subsided, but only somewhat. I felt it a few weeks later when I returned to the athletic club. I tried shooting baskets in the empty gym, but I limped on my gimpy hip with every step. It took many months, almost a year, for the discomfort to dissipate.

Never again would I venture onto icy sidewalks without grippers.

These lessons suggested that I'm no longer young and that I should not ignore ideas for avoiding falls. Not only that but, just days after I got that pamphlet, my son slipped and fell down the icy stairs outside the club. Fortunately, he suffered only a sprained ankle.

Still, one more narrow escape came to mind. The first blanket of snow had fallen one winter, and I had yet to remove an angle piece to our downspout that funneled water down the driveway. Leaving it would create an ice patch all winter.

I picked up my socket set, opened it and was considering which socket to use for this quick task as I stepped outside. While walking toward the spout, I forgot about a rope we keep hooked next to the door to let Molly out on.

As I gazed at the sockets, not thinking about the rope, I tripped over it and went flying, crashing to the driveway. Sockets scattered everywhere, some falling into the snow-covered bushes.

Other than a few minor scrapes and bruises, I escaped injury. But I'd bent my glasses and ripped a hole in the knee of a new pair of jeans. And I didn't find all of the sockets to my set until the snow melted.

I was glad no one was driving by at the time. It must have looked like some pratfall from an old-time cartoon, maybe "FogHorn LegHorn" or "Roadrunner." Or, had someone been filming it, my tumble would have been a perfect scene to submit to "America's Funniest Home Videos."

And while I can chuckle about it now, the risks of falls are no laughing matter.

35
I'd Be "Bearly" Fast Enough

The signs in Maryland's Mount Davis State Park were ominous: Beware of bears. At the trailhead, that warning included suggestions for what to do if you encounter a bear while hiking.

Cheryl and I saw similar signs a day earlier while hiking and enjoying the falls at Deep Creek State Park with our friends Dan and Nancy, not far from where they spend their summers on Deep Creek Lake, the largest lake in western Maryland. However, on that day in 2011, we saw no signs of bears.

I'd chuckled at the signs. I never considered Maryland a rural state, ripe for bears and other dangerous creatures. Instead, Maryland being adjacent to Washington, D.C., our nation's capital, I figured we'd spot more donkeys and elephants than anything. Heck, even Dan was a Pentagon retiree.

Now, Cheryl and I were hiking by ourselves on a well-worn trail leading up Mount Davis. During our walk, we spotted another ominous sign: A live bear trap. I silently considered why wildlife managers might be trying to bait and trap a bear: Because some bruin had gotten too cozy or too dangerous around humans.

Suddenly, I spotted movement on the path ahead of us and instinctively reached back with an open hand to warn my wife.

"What?" she said.

"A bear," I whispered.

"Where?"

"On the trail, dead ahead."

We stood as still as the adjacent trees while the large black bear lumbered toward us, sniffing the air. I knew that trying to outrun a bear was futile—they're too fast. Likewise, they can climb trees, so scaling one was out of the question. No buildings were nearby to offer an escape, and we were more than a mile from our car.

The bear kept coming until it was twenty yards away, then it veered off of the path into the woods as if it never knew we were present.

I crept forward.

"What are you doing?" Cheryl whispered in an annoyed tone.

"Trying to get a good picture of it, whaddya think?"

Cheryl grabbed my belt from behind and tugged, refusing to let me venture closer. In the canopy of trees, I managed only marginal photos of the beast, though good enough to confirm that, yes, we were in the company of Ursus americanus.

Soon, the bear disappeared into the woods, and Cheryl and I continued our hike unscathed.

Later, we rejoined Dan and Nancy back on their deck. Rocking in deck chairs, we sipped cocktails and contemplated a dip in their hot tub while gazing at the lake. Suddenly, in the miniature forest of tall trees and groundcover between us and the water, we spotted a young bear roaming the shoreline. I grabbed my camera and slipped down a narrow path through the foliage, again getting only marginal shots.

"You're pretty gutsy," Nancy said upon my return.

"Most anything for a good photo," I said. "Besides, as I told Cheryl out on that trail today, 'I don't have to outrun the bear; I only have to outrun you!'"

36
Keep the Faith: Packer Fans Are Everywhere

"Dang it," I said, "I screwed up in planning for this trip."

"How's that?" Cheryl said.

"I didn't think about tonight's Packer game."

It was Sept. 18, 2016, and we had already visited the Biltmore Mansion in Asheville, N.C., then drove to Bryson City, where we hiked in the Smokies. Later, we enjoyed Chattanooga, Memphis, and Nashville before arriving in Louisville, the second-to-last stop on our itinerary.

Though we stayed in a hotel across the Ohio River in Jeffersonville, Indiana, we considered Louisville the crown jewel of our vacation because we timed the trip around seeing horse races at Churchill Downs, home of the Kentucky Derby.

"The Packers play the Vikings tonight in Minnesota," I said. "How are we going to watch the game when we're out of state?"

"Maybe we can find a bar where they have the game on," she said.

"I doubt it, but we can try. I'll talk to the concierge."

At least we weren't at a Motel 6. Instead, I'd booked the well-appointed Fairfield Inn & Suites by Marriott, which offered free shuttles across the bridge into Louisville and back whenever we called for a ride.

"The Green Bay Packers are playing tonight," I told the concierge. "Do you know of any Packer bars around here?"

"Let's see," he said, tapping his computer keyboard. "There's a website, packerseverywhere.com, that lists Packer bars around the nation."

My optimism surged. I was impressed that he knew that but felt stupid that I didn't.

"Yes, here's one," he said. "Saints Pizza & Pub at 131 Breckenridge Lane in Louisville. It's seven and a half miles from here."

"Hmm, I'm new at using a cell phone for navigation," I said.

"I can print out directions, if that would help."

"That'd be great!" I said, and walked away enthused after tipping him generously.

Still, the name of the place didn't sound all that grand. I envisioned some hole-in-the-wall tavern, dim, grimy, and still acrid from the days of indoor smoking.

Cheryl and I arrived without problem, but parking was a tad tricky. We found a spot around the corner from the place.

Stepping inside a half hour before kickoff, it was evident this was an attractive sports bar, but I didn't notice any big screens tuned to the Packer pregame show. A bouncer met us near the door.

"I understand this is a Packer bar," I said.

He pointed a thumb toward a nearby stairway. "The whole second floor is reserved for Green Bay fans during Packer games," he said.

"Wow. That's cool!"

We headed upstairs, where fifteen or twenty fans had already assembled. Several bartenders scurried around a large semicircular bar that took center stage. Big-screen TVs filled every angle for fans. And speaking of stages, an actual stage on one end sported a couch and comfortable chairs.

Cheryl and I found seats on the couch. But not for long.

"Excuse me," a fellow clad in Packer green and gold soon said. "You two are sitting in our spots."

"What?" I said. "I don't understand."

"We come here for every Packer game. The regulars know that these are our spots."

"Oh," I said, not willing to make waves with a fellow fan. "Sorry. We didn't know."

"That's okay," he said as we got up and he and a buddy plopped down.

Cheryl and I found seats nearby, where we soon struck up a conversation with another couple, who lived in the area.

"So how did you come to be Packer fans?" I asked.

"I used to live in Stevens Point," the guy said. "And when we got married, she joined the bandwagon."

Soon the game was underway, as were loud and boisterous cheers. Unlike in a stadium, where fans try to hold it down when the home team's quarterback calls signals before a play, there was no need for silence here. Still, I almost felt like telling my fellow revelers to keep it down as Aaron Rodgers barked the signals.

The food was good, the beer was cold, and the bartenders were prompt. But the best part was yet to come. When the Packers scored a touchdown, an older fellow jumped on stage, football in hand, spiked the ball and did a little jig as if he just reached the end zone.

Cheryl and I roared with approval.

That happened twice.

Unfortunately, our cheers didn't last. The place took on an eerie quiet as dejected fans filed down the stairs and out the door after those pesky Vikings prevailed, 17-14, leaving Green Bay's record at 1-1.

The Vikings couldn't keep our Packers down, however. After stumbling to a 4-6 start to the season, Green Bay went on a six-game winning streak and clinched the NFC North Division for the fifth time in six years.

Even better, the Packers eliminated those despised Vikings from playoff contention with a 38-25 win in Week 16 at Lambeau Field.

Watching from the comfort of our own couch back in Janesville, we could imagine the raucous crowd—and the old guy spiking the ball—six hours to the south at Saints Pizza & Pub.

37
Retrieving a Wedding Gift in the Nick of Time

For years, Cheryl has been buying perennials—mostly irises and lilies—from "Nancy the Flower Lady" at the downtown Janesville Farmers Market. Stopping to look over Nancy's stock, in every color of the rainbow, and chat with her has become an almost weekly ritual each summer.

Knowing I am a writer and worked at *The Janesville Gazette*, Nancy shared a story about a wedding gift she and her husband received years ago.

An older couple, relatives of Nancy's husband, gave the newlyweds a handmade clock. Made of an irregular slice of wood from the base of a tree, it looks like a dark starfish minus a couple of appendages. Several coats of varnish sealed this work of art. The couple carefully packaged it in a box that once held a portable grill purchased from Kmart.

That's where things went awry. After their June ceremony, the newlyweds left for a month-long honeymoon. Upon returning, they got together with their parents to open the wedding presents. They tore the wrapping paper off this particular gift, saw the box illustrating a portable charcoal grill, and didn't open it.

"I said, 'Oh, that's nice,'" Nancy recalled. "You could not tell that the box had been opened. It looked factory sealed."

Nancy and her husband already had such a grill; they didn't need two of them. So, they did the logical thing. They returned the box—unopened—to Kmart. The store clerk gave them the money for the grill without checking inside the box.

After Nancy sent thank-you letters, including one to the couple she thought had given them a grill, her mother-in-law called to explain that it hadn't been a grill in that box but instead a handcrafted clock.

Time was ticking, so Nancy raced back to Kmart, hoping to find the box still on a shelf. Unfortunately, it was already gone.

"It was getting late in the summer, and they must have had a big clearance sale on those grills," Nancy said. "I felt just terrible."

The only thing they could think to do was call *The Gazette*—my longtime employer—and tell their tale of woe in hopes that whoever bought the grill box with the clock might return it.

The Gazette printed a story, and the newlyweds waited and hoped.

A few days later, "I got a phone call," Nancy said, "and it was this guy, and he said, 'I'm calling about the clock.' I said, 'Oh great, you got it!' He said, 'Yes, and how much is it worth to you?'

"I thought, oh my gosh, this person is trying to take advantage of me. I said, 'Well, it was a wedding gift and I feel really bad,' and I started rambling and he could tell that I was very upset.

"He said 'Do you know who this is?' And I said, 'No.'"

Turns out, it was Nancy's first cousin, the son of her mother's sister.

"I was just teasing you," he told Nancy.

He and his buddies go fishing and camping, and each person brings something for the gathering. One guy said he'd bring a grill. They were all famished after a day of fishing, so you can imagine their reaction when that fellow popped open the grill box and brought out the clock.

"They were all quite upset, except for my cousin," Nancy explained. "He said, 'I really like that clock. I'll buy it from you.'"

He gave the guy the same amount he'd paid for what he thought was a charcoal grill.

"He called my aunt that night and said, 'Oh, you won't believe this beautiful clock.' She just laughed and said, 'I'm sorry to tell you this, but do you know whose clock this is?' he said, 'It's mine,' and she said, 'Well, not really,' and she told him about the story she read in *The Gazette*."

Nancy reimbursed him what he had paid for it and got the clock back, this time for good. She called *The Gazette* to report the good news, that the missing clock had been returned to its rightful owners, but odd as it might seem, the newspaper didn't pursue a follow-up story.

"It's just so funny that my cousin ended up with it," she said. "I still have the clock, and it's still working."

Meanwhile, at fishing camp, where storytelling is as important as the daily catch, those fishing buddies have a time-honored tale to recount for years to come.

38
Free-for-All at the Little Free Library

My son laughed when I put up a Little Free Library.

"People will probably be putting beer cans and other trash in it," Josh said.

"Why wouldya think that?"

"You know how people are."

"I think you're wrong."

When I first read about the Little Free Library phenomenon, I put it on my retirement bucket list. I figured I could find a weather-proof design on the homepage of this "world's largest book-sharing movement."

However, I never got the chance to build one. Fred McCann, a friend from church and retired World War II veteran, had stopped driving, and we gave him rides to monthly breakfast gatherings. He had a woodworking shop in his garage and loved to tinker. The newspaper told how he'd built and donated three Little Free Libraries to downtown public sites.

"Would you like a Little Free Library?" he asked one day when we dropped him off.

"Sure," I said, knowing Cheryl had concerns about such a unit, concerns I didn't share or even understand.

So, he built one for us, and I bought a post to mount it on the terrace of our corner lot. I painted it white and bought a stencil to add in orange lettering "Little Free Library" and "Take a book; Leave a book."

My son was wrong. My Little Free Library has worked as intended. Adults stop. Kids stop. Families stop. One time I saw an adolescent sitting on the adjacent sidewalk, reading a book. Cheryl wouldn't budge at my suggestion we add a bench next to the library box.

Sometimes this little box of books gets crowded; other times the offerings are thin and I find a rummage sale where I can buy a few novels at a dollar apiece to replenish the supply. Once a mother down the street gave me a box of children's books to feed into it after they failed to sell at her rummage sale. Another time Cheryl and I arrived home to find a grocery bag full of books in our driveway with a note "For your Little Free Library." I still don't know who dropped them off.

For the most part, my Little Free Library has been a hit in our neighborhood.

Our Little Free Library did, however, lead to a problem. It was summertime. Our two grandkids were visiting, and we had the front door open, only the screen door separating us from the mild evening air. We were watching television when I heard kids' voices outside.

Just as I peered out the screen door to investigate, a kid hurled a book, its pages fluttering, out in the street. Other volumes already dotted the pavement.

Despite being barefoot, I sprang out the door shouting. "Hey, knock it off!"

Some of the kids had bikes, jumped on them, and pedaled off. Two more ran off on foot. Two younger kids, a boy and girl, stood paralyzed in fear as I scampered toward them.

"Who's throwing the books?" I demanded.

"Um, my brother...well, not him, but a guy with us," the boy stammered.

"What's this boy's name?" I said as I gathered the scattered books.

"Um, I don't know."

"You're trying to tell me you're hanging out with kids on the street at 9 o'clock at night and you don't know their names?"

"Well, um, we just met them," he said.

"What's your brother's name?"

"Um, Darren."

"And where do you live?"

"Um, Martin Road."

"Okay," I said, knowing Martin Road was three blocks away. "You wait right there, and I'm going to get my shoes on and take you home."

As soon as I stepped inside, however, these final two suspects took off running.

Now I was really mad.

I got my shoes on and raced for the garage and my car. I sped down the street in the direction they'd all scattered. I figured I'd catch them on Ruger Avenue, a thoroughfare, before they turned onto Martin.

But I saw nothing. All was quiet on Ruger, as well as Martin. However, a Martin Road homeowner had let his dog out, so I pulled over.

"Say," I said, "do you happen to know two brothers, maybe six and eight years old, one of them named Darren, who live on this street?"

"I think there's a couple of brothers that age who live in that house with the trailer in the driveway." He pointed toward the next block, and from frequent dog walks, I knew which house he was talking about. One with lots of kids and lots of battered adult toys and scattered children's toys.

I drove down, pulled over, and knocked. A man came to the door. "Can I help you?"

"Do you have a couple of sons maybe six and eight, one named Darren?"

"Yah, why?"

"Well, I just caught them tossing books out of my Little Free Library, and they took off running."

"What? They're supposed to be staying overnight with a friend across town."

"Well, I've got news for you buddy. They're not across town. I live three blocks from here."

"Just a minute," he said, pulling a cell phone from his pocket. He punched buttons with a fury. "Where are you?" he demanded when a son answered. "Well, you stay right there. I'm on my way."

He shoved the phone in his pocket. "Where's Fremont?"

"It's two blocks away, one block from my place," I said.

"I'll follow you," he said, heading for his car.

We found his sons standing outside a house around the corner from my home. The father angrily ordered his boys to stand by his car as we headed for the door. I rang, and a dog with a head the size of a basketball emerged and woofed before a man came to the door.

"What's up?"

"Do you have some kids, maybe one of them a girl, who've been out and about with those two out by the curb?" I said.

He gazed out at the two boys. "Yes."

"Well, I have a Little Free Library on the corner of Blackhawk and Eastwood, and I caught these kids pitching the books into the street a few minutes ago."

"Just a minute," he said, and soon returned, pushing two kids in front of him. "Are these the two?"

"I believe so," I said.

"I'll take care of this," he said, and closed the door on us.

The first father turned and began lecturing his kids in a loud, gruff, animated manner. When he paused to catch his breath, he turned to me and said, "Let me know what the damage is, and I'll make sure it's paid for."

"Well," I said, "it's a Little Free Library. These are used books, so it's hard to put a dollar value on any damage. But I'll check them over and let you know."

Turns out the books suffered no terrible damage—no torn off covers or torn out pages—but I figured that father deserved an explanation and his sons needed a lesson, so I stopped to see him the next day.

"My kids are getting out of control," he said. "I work out of town a lot, and my wife has a hard time handling them. I might have to change jobs."

"Sorry to hear that."

"Thanks," he said. "And thanks for letting me know."

Later that day, Cheryl and I were enjoying beers on our back deck when the doorbell rang. I went to answer it as my 14-year-old granddaughter listened from around the corner. There stood the brother and sister from the Fremont house.

"We came to apologize," the girl said sheepishly. "We're sorry we were throwing your books around."

"Well," I said, "If you'd spend a little more of your free time in the summer picking up a book to read instead of looking for mischief, you wouldn't be standing here apologizing."

"Yes, sir," the boy said.

"Try to stay out of trouble," I said, and they turned to leave.

I shut the door as my granddaughter stumbled out of her hiding spot, laughing to the point of falling down.

"Oh, my God," she said. "That was just like eighth grade all over again!"

39
Ease Is Not in the Bag

"What took you so long?" my wife asked.

"I'd have been back long ago, but I couldn't open those damn plastic bags again!"

"You're kidding."

"No joke. It's ridiculous. Each time I go get groceries, I'd like to drag a produce employee along to open those bags for me."

"Come on, how bad can it really be?"

"I'm serious. Last month, I was struggling with a bag when this lady pulled up with her cart—I swear she wasn't coming on to me—and explained that, 'If you pull on the little fold along these top carrying loops, it will open easier.'"

"Did that help?"

"Not much! I still end up cursing and ready to kick the cantaloupe bin. If I didn't have to wrestle with those bags, I could cut my time in that department in half. But, maybe for the store, that's the whole point."

I sense I'm not alone in my frustration. In a nation that put a man on the moon more than 50 years ago and is considering manned exploration of Mars, wouldn't you think some savvy engineer could design a plastic bag that opens simply?

Apparently not.

Or maybe it's just that, at a certain age, around your late 50s, dexterity in a man's fingers evaporates like hopes for regular bowel movements, strong and steady pee streams, and erectile function. Suddenly, it's like I'm trying to open a plastic bag with a pair of bricks.

And it's not just produce bags. Oh, no.

As I write this, our kitchen has a bag of cereal and a sleeve of crackers that failed to open with simple tugs at the sealed tops. Instead, after my exasperated pulling, these ripped down the sides. Before we consume them, they'll be as stale as week-old bagels. Frustrating!

I just signed up for Medicare, but this problem first cropped up a decade ago. I was trying to open a ziplock bag of artificial fishing bait in a scented solution. I tore off the top plastic strip, but I couldn't get my fingers between the remaining slivers of plastic to tug open the ziplock. Cursing failed to help.

In exasperation, I risked a trip to the emergency room by digging into the abyss at the bottom of my tackle box and pulling out my filet knife. By some miracle, I used the knife tip to pry open this bait bag without need to dial 911. But then, try that in a boat rocked by whitecaps.

These days, however, I find that getting those ziplocks to pull open and reseal is almost as infuriating as opening those aforementioned produce bags. Many of these products say "New E-Z open packaging." I have a bag of raisins with a ziplock that was so frustrating that when I tugged on it, the closing feature tore off of one side of the bag, rendering it useless. I had an identical problem with a bag of raisin bran. Even now, the raisins are getting hard, and the cereal is getting stale.

It's not just bags, however. Recently, while trying to pry off the corner tab on a plastic tub of chicken salad, I managed to impale my thumb. Blood spewed as I dug through a cluttered bathroom cabinet to locate the Band-Aid box.

It's as if the brilliant minds in plastic packaging industries sit in their research labs day after day, plotting revenge on their doddering grandparents who refused them those trips to the circus, the park, or even the candy store.

I imagine they're chuckling right now.

Well, I've gotta run. Next on my to-do list is taking an allergy pill, if I can extract it from one of those flat foil sheets by snaring a tiny pull corner. I'm hoping I'll still have time to mow the lawn today.

40
It's the Curse of Christmas

"At your age, you shouldn't be up on ladders anymore," my fishing buddy Bill chastised me before Christmas a few years ago.

He wasn't trying to be naughty but, rather, nice. After all, I had reached Social Security age. "Why not?" I replied.

"I know a guy who fell off a ladder. He'll never be the same."

I'd stay off ladders, too, if I were Bill. In the summer of 2021, he fell not off of a ladder but on stone steps while on vacation and broke his elbow, which bloodied his hotel sheets.

That November, I was again climbing ladders. But I struggle to explain why I still decorate our home for the holidays. The job does nothing to put me in the Christmas spirit. I should instead be checking on our church's confession schedule so I can atone for the cursing this annual frustration causes.

Decorating to thrill our two grandkids was once part of my motivation, but in December 2021, Lexi turned 20. Her brother, Remy, hit 13 a few weeks later. They're past the point of being easily impressed. Besides, we celebrated that Christmas at their home in Illinois, so they didn't even see the lights of my labor.

Still, in mid-November, I watched the extended forecasts and pored through advertising flyers pitching strings of new LED lights, wreaths, and plump little Santas. I couldn't run extension cords across the lawn too early, lest I inadvertently chop them while mulching the last leaves falling from our two stubborn maples.

Wanting to help slow climate change, I'd switch to energy-efficient icicle lights, even at considerable upfront cost. Yet these seem to only come in long strings—17 or 18 feet or more. Our home needs three long strings and at least one short one. We have a beautiful stone and brick chimney—one requiring that I defy buddy Bill and climb a ladder to attach a lighted star, which can be seen from afar. But the chimney isolates a short section of gutter for icicle lights on one end of our house.

This complication came up several years ago when we spent Thanksgiving weekend up north with Mom. I started decorating early the next week. Despite dreading the project, I dug through the massive box of decorations and snarls of tiny lights, tangled as if by mischievous elves, even though I bag each string separately. In the warm and cozy confines of my basement, I tested each set. It's almost as sure as winter snow in Wisconsin that half of some set won't light, no matter how the manufacturer guarantees that "others stay on even if one goes out." Using a knife tip—risking a trip to the emergency room—to pry open the tiny pocket and change the even tinier fuses always proves futile.

That year, all seemed to work, so I pulled out the 18-foot extension ladder and again gambled life and limb and frozen fingers to climb and attach the strings to gutters and shingles using little fasteners. After storing away the ladder, the timers clicked on and—sure enough—one half of one string was out. Not on a gutter eight feet off the ground, but one rounding the tall peak.

Mumbling and grumbling and cursing my plight, I drove to the hardware store where I'd purchased the sets two years earlier. Already sold out for the season.

More mumbling and grumbling and stumbling back to the car, I drove to Walmart, which had long strings of "cool" white lights but the only short sets featured "warm, soft" lights.

I bought them anyway. The contrast is almost as stark as having two different colors.

Of course, rather than tossing the old strings, I gazed at the new fence on our lot line and thought, gee, wouldn't those lights look lovely against those white pickets? And so each season's holiday decorating just expanded.

Last up are the two white wooden deer. They're looking weather worn; like a pair of Santa's aging reindeer ready to be freed to run the forest. I place them as far back in our side yard as possible, where they're somewhat protected from winds that rocket around the corner of our garage and too often topple these reindeer despite tent stakes holding their feet to the frozen turf. Sometimes, unless we get early winter rains, the spotlight illuminating them will even stay on.

In 2021, I had no more than hung the lights when my back seized up and one section of a long string on the peak went out. I checked Wal-Mart's website, which seemed to indicate that my local store still had the lights in stock. But after fighting traffic in Janesville's chaotic commercial corridor to reach the store, I found those shelves empty. Empty!

Returning home, I pulled out the ladder and made my way to the trouble spot, using caution lest I further aggravate my aching back. Climbing the ladder, I found all the bulbs secure. I jiggled the string repeatedly. Nothing. Finally, with one last shake, like the miracle of a virgin birth, it flicked back on.

I climbed down and was carrying the ladder on the sidewalk when I gazed up. The problematic string was again black. Cursing, I went back up on the ladder, shook and shook the section, and finally it blinked on. I got down, removed the ladder, and peered up. Still lit. I put the ladder away and thought I'd best grab a cell phone photo before it went out.

I pulled my cell phone from my pocket, but the string went dark the moment I glanced at it. "Screw it," I said, skipped the photo, and retreated to the warmth of our house. Later, while grilling supper, I again peeked up. The string was back on. Why? I don't know, but I quickly snapped a photo. Almost against all odds, that balky section stayed on for days on end. With friends due to visit for a holiday gathering a week later, I looked at the lights, and that section had again gone dark. It blinked on and off throughout the holidays as if controlled by the Grinch toying with an unknown switch.

My struggles with fickle lights bring to mind the light show at Janesville's Rotary Botanical Gardens. In December 2021, the twenty acres of gardens glowed with 1 million lights. Let that sink in a minute. I can't get a thousand to stay lighted—many of you reading probably spend holidays cursing atop similarly wobbly ladders—and somehow,

Once decorated, our home looks as pretty as a Christmas card—if all the strings stay lighted, that is.

some way, these botanical gardens keep enough lights sparkling to be spotted from outer space.

One gardens volunteer, Ron Parsons of Milton, spends summers repairing decorations. I interviewed Ron for a story in *Our Wisconsin* magazine and learned how he fixes such strings. Me? I don't have the patience. I'd rather fix problematic light sets at the bottom of my trash can.

Oh, sure, when it's done, our house looks as pretty as a Christmas card, which we had printed and sent to friends and family one year. It's gratifying to imagine the smiles and oohs and aahs aboard busloads of senior citizens that round the corner of our otherwise quiet neighborhood during an annual citywide tour of decorations.

And then I think of our neighbors, Tim and Marlene, across the street and their little granddaughter Zia, who's as cute as an elf and visits us often because she's the most social preschooler I've ever met. I imagine our decorative lights twinkling in Zia's glowing, cherubic face and think, well, maybe one more year.

41
Detective Apprehends Golf Club Thief

One Monday morning a few years ago, my good friend Dave Janisch and I were approaching Hole 5 of the north nine at Evergreen Golf Club in Elkhorn when I realized my seven iron was missing.

"Dang it," I said. (Perhaps I used a more profane word.)

"What's the matter?"

"I'm missing my seven iron. I musta left it beside that par three green a couple of holes back. I used it to chip on."

After finishing Hole 5, we circled back to talk to two groups behind us, hoping someone spotted the club and picked it up. None did.

We flagged down the ranger, who was cruising the course in a golf cart. Dave knew the guy coached basketball for Palmyra High School when he and I played at differing times for Marshall's varsity. Dave struck up a conversation with him before we'd even teed off.

"I'll zip back to that hole and see if I can find it," the ranger said, "and if not, I'll check with other groups behind you."

"Thanks," I said.

I knew I'd miss my trusty seven iron. When I was an adolescent, an old wooden-handled seven iron was the lone club in our garage. I used it to whack wiffle balls around our yard, sometimes leaving divots in Dad's lawn.

I remembered a time when my iron shots were so erratic that I pulled the seven out of my bag and methodically worked my way up most every fairway. But lately, it had become less reliable, especially if I used it to target a par 3 green. My ball might slice right, might duck hook left. I couldn't predict it. As they say, hide the women and children.

It doesn't help that my diverse interests and family commitments limit my golf time to a few outings per season, whereas Dave, a former city detective and now a private eye, gets out weekly. I might win a hole or two, but he'll score around ten shots better for each nine.

Of course, I wasn't the one who hit the hotel as we approached a green at Four Seasons near Pembine, but that's another story.

On this day, however, my seven iron had helped me chip onto that Hole 3 after my tee shot escaped the marsh and pond nearby.

Dave and I completed our round and flagged down the ranger one last time.

"Any luck finding that club?"

"Nope," he said. "But you might wanna check that little ranger station near the clubhouse. Golfers sometimes return clubs there."

"Thanks, I will."

When we pulled up to the building, looking much like a phone booth or one of those buildings rural homeowners build to keep schoolkids warm while awaiting the bus, no one was there. But I found lots of missing clubs of all shapes and sizes. Just not the seven iron that matched my set.

Returning to the clubhouse, I wrote down the brand of clubs—Paradigm head with a Golfsmith black Carbon Stick handle—and jotted my name and phone number. I handed my note to the attendant.

"I hope you get it back," he said.

"Me, too!"

A week passed, then another. I called the golf club.

"Nope, no one turned in such a club," I was told.

I couldn't believe it. Golf is supposedly a gentlemen's game. Who the heck would pick up and keep someone else's club? Wouldn't the person already have a decent seven iron in his or her bag? What would be the point of not turning it in?

I fumed.

Weeks passed before Dave and I got a chance to align our schedules and return for another outing at Evergreen.

We paid our green fees, grabbed a cart, and hit the parking lot to gather our golf bags.

That's when Dave pulled a seven iron—my seven iron—out of his bag.

"Where the hell didya find that?" I asked.

"It was in my bag all along," he said with a smile.

Obviously, Dave had collected my club after that Hole 3, stuck it in his bag without thinking, and never realized he had it until a subsequent outing.

Quite the detective, that Dave. A superman among sleuths.

42
Yes, It's Called Yard Work, So Get Busy

I don't know what it is with many homeowners today, particularly young ones.

Say what you will about the elderly—sure, lump me into that collective—but we know a few things about life. These include how to maintain a yard and home. Meanwhile, many in the younger generation can't be bothered.

How do I know? Because I'm a creature of habit. Every morning, I walk our dog, Molly, a mile. And I'm habitually annoyed by too many residents in this extended neighborhood.

You know the types.

First and foremost, there's the litter—beer cans, water bottles, and fast food refuse lying on lawns and terraces and in streets. I realize that most of this stuff gets tossed by passing motorists or pedestrians. But many homeowners can't see past the ends of their driveways. When they roll those bins to the curb on trash day, can't they collect this rubbish and toss it in? No, so I often do it for them.

Litter isn't the only problem. Some lawns look like jungles. The city says lawns should be no taller than twelve inches. I can point out one that gets mowed about as often as the city's street sweeper comes around.

Weeds and hedges crowd sidewalks and threaten passersby. Woe to the person in a wheelchair trying to get past those protruding hedges.

The city also says branches should be seven feet above the sidewalk. Why? Because when trees get wet, those limbs sag and force people to do the limbo. Walkers risk their eyesight when strolling at night.

People also leave fallen tree limbs lying around their yards or on sidewalks. The next time one guy on my walk uses a broom to sweep grass clippings off his sidewalk will be the first time. Meanwhile, the debris threatens to swallow the entire concrete walkway.

Some homeowners ignore dangerously cracked or shifted sidewalk slabs until someone files a complaint and the city gets around to ordering repairs.

Don't get me started on those who neglect to clear sidewalks of ice and snow in winter, despite a city ordinance requiring prompt attention. I've taken more than one nasty spill.

There's more. Much more. Too many people leave trash bins standing sentinel at the curb two or even three days after collection. Others can't seem to find their driveways while pulling in, leaving tire ruts and unsightly, muddy messes for sidewalk users to step around. I've seen junk cars, including one in the street that smelled of leaking gas for weeks. Some residents park their cars on lawns or think next-door neighbors want to gaze out at trailers perennially parked between homes on narrow lots.

I once pointed out these annoyances to my boss at the newspaper. He called me anal.

Suggesting I've become a curmudgeon, a high school classmate read one of my rants on Facebook and concurred with my boss.

Choose your cliché:

"Let it go."

"Relax."

"Take a chill pill."

"Serenity now."

"Let it be."

"Not your next-door neighbor? Then it's not your problem."

I realize I'm generalizing; some younger homeowners keep their yards neat and tidy, while some older folks are too frail to get the jobs done, too poor to hire help, or could care less.

Regardless, why do I care so much about yard care? First, keeping your yard, home, and sidewalks in good shape is courteous, polite, and neighborly. Second, neglect reflects poorly on the entire neighborhood. It's like the policing theory that suggests one broken window can lead to decay of an entire block. Then, crime won't be far behind.

There goes property values. Yours and mine.

So if you want to live like you're out in the country, where your next-door neighbor might be a cornfield away, move there!

Thanks for helping me get this off my chest. Call me crotchety, label me anal, but I feel better already.

Still, when the day comes that Molly heads off to that big dog park in the sky, and Dear Spouse and I decide to get another pup, I think we should name it Peeve.

That's right. Then, each morning, I'll be walking my pet, Peeve.

Seems fitting, doesn't it?

43
Serving Breakfast and Warm Smiles

For many years, I helped serve morning meals to kids at Janesville's Roosevelt School, and when the district disbanded the breakfast clubs at Roosevelt and six other elementary schools, it left a sour taste in the mouths of hundreds of volunteers.

I started volunteering after encouragement from an older coworker, who served meals with her church at Roosevelt. Helping out made sense because my son, Josh, was attending Roosevelt. A handful of churches rotated a week at a time, and when I learned ours was among them, I switched to helping fellow parishioners from St. John Vianney Catholic Church. I was still working at *The Gazette* full time, but I wasn't punching a time clock, and arriving a little later than usual one week each month didn't bother anyone.

We understood the program's benefits because more than a third of children lived in impoverished homes, but longtime Roosevelt Principal Lynn Karges emphasized the value, as well. The school hosted year-end thank-you breakfasts for volunteers, and Karges told stories—without naming names—that brought many of us to tears. She explained that, because one girl's parents had no car, she couldn't get to school on time until the school made arrangements. One boy arrived for breakfast early, and his reading skills improved after a volunteer suggested he bring a book to fill the extra time.

When the program ended just before Christmas in 2012, I was still the youngest among St. John Vianney volunteers and the only one still working. My son had graduated high school more than a decade earlier.

Then-Superintendent Karen Schulte made all sorts of excuses for dropping the breakfast clubs in favor of the federally funded Universal Free Breakfast program.

First, the federal money would help feed children at four more schools where students previously paid to eat. Schulte reasoned that more kids would eat breakfast because the meals were no longer considered just for the poor.

Second, the federal guidelines would better control nutrition. Sure, some donated cereals the volunteers served were heavy on sugar, but the breakfast clubs made changes when requested. For example, we switched from serving 2 percent milk to 1 percent milk.

Sanitation and safety were expressed as additional concerns. True, volunteers underwent no training in food service, yet we mainly fed toast, cereal, and the occasional oatmeal. No one could point out a case of a child falling ill from eating those meals.

Finally, Schulte noted the district had little control over the volunteers, who underwent no background checks. But again, no one could point to a case of some pervert volunteering just for the chance to molest a child.

Maybe, in hindsight, it was a wise move because, well, COVID.

Back then, however, the most disheartening thought for volunteers was the fact that we learned how much some of those impressionable youngsters needed not just breakfast but warm smiles and encouraging words. Some students gobbled down bowls of cereal and miniature mountains of toast as if they hadn't eaten since the school lunch the day before. But many kids were hungry not just for food but for attention. Some came from troubled homes, and in our modern era of mobility, many kids didn't have consoling grandparents nearby. Volunteers, then, most of them elderly, served not just food but as surrogate grandparents.

One boy at Roosevelt came rather scruffy looking and with a bad attitude almost daily. I remembered my interview with a police liaison officer at another elementary school. We were walking the halls as class was about to begin, and a child raced up to him.

"Officer Sullivan, is my dad okay?"

"Yes, yes, he's fine."

"Did he get his medicine?"

"Yes, he got his medicine."

The distress in the boy's face dissipated, and he hurried off to class. Sullivan turned to me and said, "We had to arrest his dad last night."

I wondered how that child could focus on learning.

This surly boy at Roosevelt apparently came from a stressful home, as well. While some volunteers hung in the kitchen, I roamed the tables, directed traffic, and interacted with kids while pouring juice or milk. This boy was among early arrivals, so I took time to sit and chat with him. I did so the next day, too, and I sensed these visits were making a difference. He didn't act out as much. Someone cared.

Through the years, I acquired a few wooden mind-bender puzzles that often stumped the kids. It wasn't all fun and games, however.

The minority kids often congregated at one table, and at times there was tension between those boys and the white kids on adjacent tables. On a late-December morning, verbal taunts descended into a scuffle. After we managed to separate the kids and the bell rang, I wound up in Principal Karges' office, trying to ID perpetrators through the yearbook from the school's previous year. Not the way I wanted to get into the Christmas spirit.

But mostly, I remember brighter interactions with the kids. For example, one little girl lived in our neighborhood, and because she was a Brownie, I bought Girl Scout cookies from her. One winter day, she arrived for breakfast with bare hands red from the frigid air.

"Where are your mittens?"

"I left them upstairs yesterday," she replied. "I'm not supposed to go up there before the bell rings. Could you come with me to get them?"

I probably wasn't supposed to escort a child upstairs, but she wanted to play outside with her schoolmates, so we went and found her mittens.

We often wore name tags, and one boy got a kick out of the fact we had the same name. Every day he'd greet me loudly, "Hi, Greg!"

"Hi, Greg!" I'd respond.

One time, as I walked through the former Boston Store at the mall, I spotted Greg sitting on a stool in the makeup department. His mother sat on another stool as a clerk applied a sample. I snuck up behind Greg and said, "Hi, Greg! Are you trying on some makeup?"

My tease made him blush, just as I intended.

My favorite interaction, however, was with a little girl with a cherubic face. Though her name has long since escaped me, she was in kindergarten and one day arrived with a question for me.

"Do cows have soft udders?"

I almost dropped my juice pitcher. Having worked summers on my uncle's dairy farm as a teenager, I knew the answer. I stammered. "What was that?"

"Do cows have soft udders?" she repeated.

"Why do you want to know that?"

"We're taking a field trip to a farm today, and someone told me cows have soft udders."

"Well, I guess they do," I replied.

The next day, I spotted her standing in the doorway, obviously reluctant to come in for breakfast. I walked over. "Good morning! Aren't you hungry?"

"I don't think I should come in," she said.

"Why not?"

"I might have cow poop on my shoes!"

"I doubt that's a problem," I said, glancing at her shoes. "Come on in."

She skipped toward the food line, a smile on her face.

Oh, the innocence of youth!

44
Sister Puts the "Ho Ho Ho" in the Holidays

My only sister, Karen, likes to send out Christmas newsletters to friends and family, including her three brothers. Such newsletters, as you know, recap the year's high points, such as a trip to Australia, construction of that vacation home on the lake, or the teen acing an ACT and heading to Harvard.

Except Karen never had kids. She is three years older than I am, and at 17, she married a Marshall man who was several years older, a guy serving in the U.S Navy. Instead, their Jack Russell terriers fill their parental needs. For one Christmas, Karen's highlight was installation of their new kitchen floor.

Through the years, Karen collected dolls, marbles, and angels. She topped one Christmas newsletter with the headline "Hark the Herald Angles Sing." Spelling was never her strong suit.

You'd think the sailor, a near genius and computer geek whose job in nuclear research involved solving lengthy mathematical equations that would make a mere mortal's head hurt, and whose hobbies include stained glass, woodworking, and online games, could have taken a break from a busy computer session to review the newsletter before Karen sent it out.

But he didn't.

One Thanksgiving, they invited the family to their home in Illinois. Penny, the female Jack Russell, was well behaved, while Sparks, the male, threatened to chew the leg off anyone who dared move. Yet Karen wouldn't think of caging the nasty critter.

When it was time to eat, we crept into the dining room and slid into our seats in front of a savory-smelling roast turkey, and the sailor pulled up an extra chair for Sparks. The sassy little snarler proceeded to sit back on his hind legs and give us an anatomical salute.

We gave our greatest thanks when it was time to leave.

By the next Christmas, Sparks had—finally—passed on to doggie hell, and Karen and the sailor replaced him with yet another male Jack Russell pup, Bean.

Karen thought Bean—whom we had yet to meet—needed agility lessons, despite our hints about behavioral classes. Given Karen's stories about Bean chewing up everything in his path, getting around seemed to be the least of his problems.

One evening, she was driving Bean to class. This in itself was a challenge. After failing her driver's test twice as a teen, Karen stopped trying until she finally passed in her 20s. No one knows how many lives that delay saved.

On this night, the glare of oncoming headlights made it difficult for Karen to see the driveway to where Bean's classes were held. She turned where she thought the drive was and negotiated a couple of sharp curves before she realized she wasn't on the driveway but on a paved *bicycle trail.*

Good thing it was dark and December. No bicyclists were in harm's way.

Ahead of her lay a wooden bridge to a parking lot where she could escape her predicament. But she didn't know if the bridge was strong enough to hold a vehicle, so Karen tried to back down the trail, only to miss the turn, slide off the pavement, and get stuck.

With her cell phone, she called home. But the guy who sailed around the world had no idea where she was.

So, Karen dialed 911.

"Exactly where are you?" a bewildered police officer asked.

The police struggled to find her, and Karen worried more about the nervous Bean than her own comfort while she awaited help.

Finally, an officer showed up, perhaps with help from a helicopter crew that spotted our stranded sister.

"Did he give you a sobriety test?" I asked as she told the story during our family's Christmas gathering.

SNAKES, SQUIRRELS & BEARS, OH MY!

"He didn't even check my license or registration," Karen said.

The officer did, however, notice she was driving a Subaru Outback with four-wheel drive. He hopped in and, after working the little SUV back and forth a few times, got it back on the pavement and drove it over the bridge to freedom.

Karen thought nothing of revealing the episode, explaining that she thought it was good to laugh at herself.

That's my sister—doing her best to put the "ho ho ho" in our holidays.

45
Reports of My Demise...

On Valentine's Day 2000, I had been working for more than a decade as Sunday editor of *The Janesville Gazette*. Each Saturday night, I oversaw a small crew applying the finishing touches, adding live news to generous feature offerings before sending to press the company's flagship newspaper. Working each Saturday meant my days off were Sunday and Monday.

That Feb. 14 was a Monday, and I was home. News clerk Donna Olson pulled a death notice from a funeral home off the fax machine and started weeping. The name? Gregory A. Peck, 42, of Lexington Drive, Janesville.

The newsroom scrambled. Other staffers failed to find someone in accounting to verify my address, age, and middle initial.

Reporter Shelly Birkelo then took bold and decisive action. She dialed my home phone number.

I answered. "Hello?"

"Oh, God, Greg! This is Shelly in the newsroom. I'm so happy just to hear your voice."

"Why's that?"

Shelly explained the faxed death notice. It obviously wasn't mine. Instead, I, Gregory M. Peck, age 43, was alive and kicking, on Eastwood Avenue, a few blocks from Lexington.

Still, the fears didn't stop there.

Switchboard operator Judy Olsen doubted it was me but began to worry when two former *Gazette* employees called her at home that night to inquire about the death notice in that day's paper.

SNAKES, SQUIRRELS & BEARS, OH MY!

John Halverson, head of our Walworth County operations, called me at home that night after Mike O'Brien from our company's radio stations had asked whether the Sunday editor had met his demise.

"Ah! You're alive!" John said when I answered.

I laughed. "You had doubts?"

"Well, not really. But O'Brien called me, concerned after seeing that death notice in today's paper."

"Believe I've heard about that one, yes," I said. "Pretty gutsy of you to call. You were probably hoping those one-on-one basketball drubbings were over."

John laughed, too.

The next day, John drove to Janesville for business in our corporate offices, and as he passed me in the hallway, he proclaimed, "Dead man walking."

I chuckled again and shook my head.

That same morning, while he was at our offices to place an obituary, funeral home director John Whitcomb, never at a loss for a joke, grabbed my wrist to check for a pulse.

"You probably thought you were in line for some business," I shot back. "Tough luck, buddy."

After that, whenever a reporter begged for a delay to a story's deadline, I had a ready response: "Hey, that guy was 42 and I'm already 43; I'm living on borrowed time. Start typing!"

Looking back on it, I have never had so many people say "Nice to see you" and really mean it.

46
A Dose of Reality

July 18:

Me ("Papa"), in a text: "Heard you got a new job! Congrats! Call me sometime; I would love to hear about it!"

Granddaughter (at age 20): "Okay! I'll give you a call soon!!"

Aug. 11:

Me: "Define 'soon.'"

Granddaughter: "When there is idle time between working a 9.5-hour workday, cleaning, making dinner, and looking for apartments. Adulthood is hard."

Me: *"Really?"*

My granddaughter, Lexi, had no idea how much she'd just said.

About the Author

Greg Peck was born in Marshall, Wisconsin, and is a 1975 graduate of Marshall High School. He earned a journalism degree from the University of Wisconsin-Oshkosh in 1979.

Peck lives in Janesville and retired in 2016 as *The Janesville Gazette's* opinion page editor. He won numerous Wisconsin Newspaper Association awards and previously worked at newspapers in Oconomowoc and Wisconsin Rapids. He joined the Wisconsin Writers Association in 2006 and served as a board member.

Other works by Peck:

"Death Beyond the Willows," the true story of a 1927 wedding day tragedy that involved a couple married in Peck's hometown of Marshall. It debuted in 2005 and was revised and published again in 2013.

"Memories of Marshall," a 2020 title about growing up in a small town. Profits from this book—nearly $5,000 so far—benefit the Marshall Area Historical Society.

Made in the USA
Monee, IL
22 May 2023

34178819R00098